DARK MESA

Ross McCall is a rounder-up of maverick cattle for his own small herd. When he provides aid to wounded bandit Ace Morgan — last surviving member of an outlaw gang, and his pa's old comrade — the dying man repays his kindness by sharing the location of the band's last haul, hastily squirrelled away on McCall's land. But others are after the loot, imprisoning McCall and searching his spread for the money. On his release, can McCall face down those who would snap up his land — and succeed in finding his legacy?

HANK J. KIRBY

DARK MESA

Complete and Unabridged

LINFORD
Leicester

First published in Great Britain in 2014 by
Robert Hale Limited
London

First Linford Edition
published 2016
by arrangement with
Robert Hale Limited
London

A catalogue record for this book is available
from the British Library.

ISBN 978–1–4448–2825–2

Published by
F. A. Thorpe (Publishing)
Anstey, Leicestershire

Set by Words & Graphics Ltd.
Anstey, Leicestershire
Printed and bound in Great Britain by
T. J. International Ltd., Padstow, Cornwall

This book is printed on acid-free paper

Prologue

Bloodbath

While the other gang members checked the loads in their guns, Ace Morgan saw to the horses, testing cinch straps and bridles.

Getaway mounts were more important than the weapons once the job had been done — and any man with half a brain always looked *beyond* that tense and exciting, not to say, *dangerous* time of the actual holdup.

In this case, the mounts were all right and he knew his guns were ready, as long as the second getaway broncs were waiting in Mushroom Canyon, *and providing there wasn't as much opposition as they were expecting, it should all go well.*

Which meant they would all be rich by sundown and that long-promised retirement would be waiting for him to enjoy in his later years. Maybe with a wife, if he could find a woman who would have him: might be a little late to expect any kids, but — maybe not. To make sure, he figured to pick a young and lusty mate.

He rolled a cigarette and lit up, watching the others. As he did, Johnny Kibbe broke away and came across.

He was known as 'Killer' Kibbe to the gang and some of the Wanted dodgers had taken up the nickname, but not many called him that to his face. The war had made him what he was: turned him into a sharp-shooter and he was damned good at it; grew to love the tension and build-up as he let his target get almost out of range before bringing him down with the long-barrelled Kruger sniper's rifle.

He held that gun now, butt to the ground between his feet, folded hands across the muzzle.

Morgan shook his head slowly. 'One of these days that damn gun's gonna blow your hands off, Johnny — and your head, too, if it's in the way.'

'Nah. Me and old Kruger' — he slapped the rifle lightly — 'are on too good terms for that. But, Ace, you *sure* about this payroll? I mean, a hundred thousand dollars! What kinda company has a payroll big as that?'

'The Shamrock Mining Company. They hit a bonanza. I got friends who tell me about these things an' they're payin' a bonus to all their workers so don't worry about it, *amigo*, it's there in the Wells Fargo Depot, waitin' for us to collect. An' better we do it there than try to get past the troop of armed guards they'll have when they move it the rest of the way by stagecoach . . . *and* they'll have it in an extra-strong box that'll take a bundle of dynamite to open. They won't expect no one to try to hit the depot itself.'

Kibbe didn't look fully convinced, but Ace Morgan had led them on plenty of successful robberies and this one had been planned with more than usual care. He shrugged and shouldered the Kruger.

'I won't need the Kruger's range this time, then.'

'No. Leave it behind. Long as Strap's got the getaway broncs in place, we'll be relaxin' in Mañana Land in two days . . . an' there'll be plenty things you won't wanna be takin' at long range there!'

Kibbe grinned and wandered off. Morgan felt the tension building in him now as he watched the others making their own silent plans. *Good men all: on equal shares* — after a double share for himself as boss . . .

The Big One. He couldn't believe his chance was here after all this time. Well, he'd spent a lot of hours planning this one and if it didn't work out he deserved to go under. They all did . . .

It simply *had* to go well. That old head wound kept giving him trouble at unexpected times and needed proper, and expensive, medical attention: this was his chance to get it.

4

But it all went wrong, just about as badly as it could.

They jumped the Wells Fargo team in the depot without a hitch, taking them completely by surprise . . . all except one man who had been out in the privy and walked in on a scene he had never even imagined.

Armed men holding up the depot! *A Wells Fargo Depot?* No one in their right mind would try such a thing!

He was game, but foolish. Right then he should have backed outside and run for help. But he was loyal and boosted by the fact that Wells Fargo paid his wages, figured because he had entered silently and the outlaws didn't appear to have noticed him, that he could get the upper hand.

What he got was a bullet in the brisket from Johnny Kibbe, always quick on the trigger at short range, as if he couldn't wait to see his target go down thrashing.

Kibbe put two more bullets into the latecomer, who twisted with the strike of lead as he instinctively fired back. It was fast, deadly shooting and Ace Morgan jerked and staggered as one of the slugs burned across his head — almost exactly on the old scar that had left him with these unbearable headaches that drove him berserk with little memory of what had happened during those violent minutes.

An old Spanish sawbones had put a metal plate over the original wound where the bullet had gouged out a few inches of protective bone, and the bullet now hit this, jarred the plate loose so that it flew across the office where the Wells Fargo men stood with hands raised under the menacing guns of the robbers.

Big Ace let go an involuntary roar that froze everyone there, all eyes snapping around to stare as he staggered, the terrible wound flooding his lower face and shoulder with bright blood. Somehow he managed to stay on his feet and, with unbearable agony tearing at his brain, swung his shotgun around to where three of the Fargo men were grouped, tensed, ready to make their try for freedom.

The blast shook the windows and the second barrel's thunder followed hard upon the first. The men were sent flying like a trio of nincpins, limbs jerking, blood spraying.

The move had startled Morgan's men for this had been planned as a job with minimum violence — surprise being the key — and now, suddenly, it was a slaughterhouse.

Morgan was roaring unintelligibly, striding about, wild-eyed, empty shotgun in one hand, Colt in the other. There was a grey-haired female clerk, and she took a chance, either from panic or misplaced bravery, snatched up a gun from the drawer in the counter where she stood. She screamed as she fired, startling the outlaws. Morgan whirled, triggered instinctively. His bullet took her in the narrow chest, flung her violently into the wall.

'That does it!' yelled Red Cousins, who was closest. 'No quarter now, boys!

If we're caught nothin'll save us!'

They all knew he was right and the remaining clerks figured they, too, had nothing to lose and reached for their own firearms. *A brief, miniature war erupted.*

Johnny Kibbe leapt forward, half-crouching, fanning his gun hammer. But he only had two bullets left and he missed both clerks. Then he lurched and danced a brief jig of death as their lead cut him down and flung him into a corner.

The clerks paid for their victory under a hail of lead from the other armed men. Bloody-faced, muttering, Morgan reloaded his shotgun, twisted and fired it one-handed, blowing a Fargo man clear through the street-front window.

At the same time, Marty Shaw yelled, 'I got it! I got the payroll!'

His voice broke with his excitement as he strained to hold up one of the well-known Wells Fargo armoured satchels with the leather-covered metal front, back and sides.

'Man, is it heavy!' he added, grunting with effort.

This news seemed to settle Morgan some although he looked a terrible, frightening figure with so much blood covering him, swaying on his feet.

'That's it, then! *Get the hell outa here!*'

Excitement ran through the ranks of the robbers and their guns blazed in final, wild enthusiasm.

'Save your lead!' Morgan yelled, staggering towards the shattered window and throwing a leg carefully over the jagged glass. 'Clear town and make for the canyon!'

'Hope Strap's got them getaway broncs ready!' someone yelled fervently, making for a side door.

'We're dead if he hasn't!' called someone else.

As it turned out, they were dead anyway when the posses that swarmed the countryside finally ran them to ground three days later. *No quarter asked or given.*

Folk swear to this day that gunsmoke

from the final shoot-out was so thick it fogged the mountain slopes as far as the base of the nearby mesa.

For the few barely living survivors there were plenty of ropes eager to toss over conveniently low branches.

They weren't even allowed to die of their wounds: they were strung up and left for the buzzards to pick over.

★ ★ ★

Yet one man lived through that bloodbath, for a while, anyway.

Just one man . . .

1

The Mesa

It was almost nightfall before Ross McCall drove the last three mavericks he had rounded up into his newly built holding ground on the higher part of the mesa. It was now becoming crowded with seven other long-horned beasts already there, welcoming — or warning — the newcomers with bellows and snorts.

'Be friends, fellers, OK?' McCall said in a low, weary voice that still reflected his satisfaction with the day's work.

These cattle, together with the dozen or so others he had roped in over the last couple of weeks and kept in Arrowhead Draw, would form the nucleus of his own herd and he would make sure his own brand, R-20 — his initial and age, the numerals within the loop of the letter — was burned deep into their hides.

He had already had reprimands from a couple of local ranchers: the 'maverick law' had never been popular with greedy, careless cowmen who didn't see to proper round-up and branding. Yet they bitched plenty when the unmarked, and thereby legally free, roaming steers were picked up by small-timers like McCall.

If it wasn't too many, most of the big men grumbled and let it go with a veiled warning that might or might not be genuine — some, perhaps, remembering their own shaky start in the beef industry in this remote area of Arizona, south of the Gila Bend and Painted Rock.

McCall wasn't too popular, in any case, around Keystone, which was one reason he spent as much time as he could on the mesa. He led his claybank down to the creek and let the animal stand belly-deep while he stripped off his shirt, doused his head in the cold water and sluiced under his arms and across his chest. He cupped hands and managed to pour a pint or two of water over his back with its small network of criss-crossed scars, souvenirs of his orphanage days. He dried his hands on the shirt and sat back against a tree trunk until the claybank waded ashore and looked at him, urging him to get down to the cabin and a nosebag of grain.

McCall grinned, stood, pulled on the shirt and as he set his battered hat with one hand, stroked the horse behind an ear. 'You get to boss me around — just this once, mind — 'cause you did such good work rounding up them steers, but don't make a habit of bein' bossy, OK?'

He drew out the last word, tensing as his gaze wandered past the claybank and downslope to the old line cabin he was fixing up to live in.

He thought he saw a speck of light — firefly, maybe? — or someone looking through the cabin by match-light! He was mildly surprised to find he was holding his rifle, hadn't even been conscious of taking it from the scabbard.

By God! There was someone in there!

He levered a shell into the breech, fully aware of what he was doing now. But he didn't mount, merely took the bridle in his left hand and led the claybank quietly down the narrow twisting trail, rifle gripped firmly, narrowed eyes watching the brief shadows now flitting across the cabin's two front windows with their raised shutters.

'Whoever you are, you're kinda careless, feller,' he told himself quietly. 'Either that, or you don't give a damn.'

His hand convulsively tightened his grip on the cocked rifle at the thought.

He stepped into the cabin doorway, rifle held in both hands now, just as the intruder touched a match to the wick of the oil lamp on the pine table. McCall squinted and said, 'Now just set down in one of them chairs and keep your hands above the table edge.'

The man spun, dropping the match, right hand streaking for his hip but — he seemed to stumble, grabbed the table with both hands. A big man, with heavy shoulders and —

Then McCall noticed the dirty, bloodstained bandage on his head, the pain-drawn face with deep-etched lines, as the bulky body twisted and fell awkwardly into the chair. The man leaned heavily against the straight-back, looking over his shoulder with trail-reddened eyes. 'S'all right, kid — I — I won't hurt you.'

'Know damn well you won't!' Ross McCall told him firmly, lifting the rifle. 'What're you doin' in my cabin?'

The man was breathing heavily and now McCall could see a large blood-stain down one side of his face and neck, passing under the edge of the collar of his torn shirt.

'You hurt bad?'

The man looked at him with those bleary eyes held steady in the pain-ravaged face.

'Pretty bad. I — I won't hang around long. They'll be here sometime soon an' I — I don't wanna get you — into trouble for harbourin' me.'

McCall was silent for long moments, then said, 'You're talkin' about a posse, ain't you?' He didn't wait for confirmation or denial, added with a rush, 'Jesus, Mary and Joseph! You — you're one of them held up the Wells Fargo place at August Creek!'

The man merely stared and just as McCall was about to speak, nodded — once.

'The last one. They done for all my men. Strung up Red Cousins even though he died an hour before. Had a hemp necktie on me, too.' He reached up with a shaking hand and pulled down the frayed collar of his shirt. McCall leaned a little closer to get a better view in the gloomy lamplight, saw the rope-burn plain enough, raw and angry-looking. 'But I managed to . . . get away.'

McCall whistled softly through his

teeth. 'You're — who?'

He was surprised when the man's bearded lips moved and he realized he was giving a silent laugh. 'I was feelin' a mite more spry, I'd likely shoot you for bein' so nosy.'

'Ace Morgan!' McCall said abruptly. 'Seen your dodger in Keystone a while back.'

'Kid, you — you wouldn't have a slug of whiskey?'

'Don't run to such luxuries. Coffee's about all I can offer — and some grub if you're up to it. You look kinda tuckered.'

'If the coffee'll eat a hole in a bucket I'll have a gallon, but I'll pass on the grub.'

He was almost falling out of the chair and McCall made his decision, lowered the rifle's hammer and stood the weapon in a corner. He took down his battered coffee tin from a shelf he'd only put up two days ago and prodded the banked fire in the battered ranch stove.

17

Morgan stiffened when he made for the door.

'Relax, gonna draw some well water for the coffee. Reckon you oughta have that head wound looked at, too. I'll fix another bandage. Hey! No arguments, OK?'

Morgan drank three cups of coffee and ate two fresh-made biscuits. He sat quietly now in the chair as McCall unwrapped the bloody bandage around his head.

'You can get yourself in a lot of trouble helpin' me this way, kid, but I 'preciate it.'

'I'll tell anyone who asks I'd do the same for a cur-dog,' McCall said, working on the wound now, as Morgan's eyebrows shot up. 'Would, too!' Then he saw the extent of the wound and sucked in air through his teeth. 'God Almighty!'

Morgan, close to exhaustion, managed a brief laugh. 'Damn! But ol' Hondo brung you up right, din' he!'

Ross McCall stiffened, looking swiftly at Morgan.

The outlaw was showing much strain now. 'We — rode together for a spell. He ever mention it?'

'Not straight out, but coupla times I picked up on things he let slip — mebbe on purpose, I dunno . . . He mentioned your name a few times.'

'Yeah. Hey, kid! Easy on that bandage! Not too tight. Ah, that's better. I come here — 'specially to see you . . .'

'Look. I ain't been on the mesa long, but I know a few hiding places — that head wound's awful. I dunno as I can do much more for it than just rebandage it, but mebbe I could get a sawbones to take a look at it.'

Morgan held up a big hand that trembled. 'No. Don't wanna involve you no more. I owe your pa for lots of things — just take my word! I'm beholden — I want to square away — I know I won't make it. Not even sure I want to with this damn head wound. The law handed your pa a rough deal when they found out who he really was, even though he was tryin' to go straight for your sake. He coulda shortened his jail sentence by givin' me and the boys away but he stayed mum. When they caught up with us, the posse thought they had the payroll satchel but it was a fake Red Cousins made up before the job. We let 'em find it and it gave us a chance to get away — me, with the real satchel.' He paused. 'I'm the only one left now.' He made a sick kind of grunt, grabbed one side of his head, looked up into McCall's face. 'Hondo done the right thing by us — and you. He quit us and went to take care of you after he heard your ma'd died and they was passin' you around the orphanages, you know?' He stopped abruptly, looking sharply at the door. 'Someone out there!'

'*Kid! You better come out!* 'Cause we're about to come in a-'smokin'!' The voice came from the now dark country-side, upslope from the cabin.

'The goddamn posse!' snapped Morgan, fumbling for his six-gun. He fired a shot through the open shutter. 'Kid's OK, but you try to move in and I'll blow his head off!'

'Hey! Take it easy!' McCall said, startled, even though Morgan winked his left eye.

McCall could hear the posse moving to surround the cabin, the lawman yelling something about Morgan not making things any worse. The outlaw was crouched under the window shutter now, checking his gun. Face like a death's head, he spoke quickly to McCall, who crouched almost beside him.

'I hid that satchel in a draw — kinda like an arrowhead — ' He gasped, short of breath, looking bad now.

'Arrowhead Draw — I use it to hold my mavericks.'

Morgan continued before McCall could say any more. 'Kid, the satchel's yours, everythin' that's in it — *Christ!* Don't gimme no arguments! Woulda been your pa's if he was still alive an' he'd've passed it on to you. Now *shut up!* You've helped me and could be in a heap a trouble for doin' it: there's only one thing I can think of might help *you.*'

McCall was pale and tense now. 'What's that?'

'This!'

Morgan's gun barrel crashed against McCall's skull and as he spun away into star-shot darkness, the outlaw shouted, 'I'm comin' out, you sons of bitches! An' you ain't takin' me alive!'

McCall spun away into a blackening gulf but heard the first hammering crash of the posse's volley, shouting as they stormed the cabin, then . . . nothing.

2

Welcome Back

'We don't serve jailbirds here, mister!'

O'Malley, the storekeeper, big-bellied and sour-looking, glared belligerently across the counter at the tall young ranny standing on the other side.

He was in from the range: that was obvious by the sun-faded hat, well-used spurs and the work-worn, badly patched clothes; a man without a woman to take care of such chores. A loner, deeply tanned, but there was also a strange hint of pallor beneath the bronze. His eyes were blue-green, looked directly at O'Malley.

'I live on the mesa. Apart from the local sheriff's hoosegow here, there ain't a jail within a hundred miles.'

His voice had a hushed sound to it, yet every word was plainly audible. Some men would know that it was a way of talking only learned after a long spell in jail . . .

'Mister, you may be a long ways from Yuma, but I know damn well you did time on the rockpile there — and before that your old man did longer. Guess it runs in the family, huh?'

The tall ranny would've liked to deny it by crashing his fist into the middle of O'Malley's large nose, but contained himself with, 'I served three year and a half. They gave me the extra six months for killin' another inmate.'

There was a challenging note in those words and they drew a sudden silence from O'Malley, but only for a moment. 'So you're a killer, too, now!'

'Kill or be killed — that's the way it is in Yuma. They decided I didn't start the fight or they'd've hanged me.'

'I'd've gone along with that! No matter, anyway, I ain't gonna serve you. You got an argument with that?'

As he spoke, the storekeeper brought up a sawn-off double-barrelled shotgun, slowly and deliberately.

Looking mighty wary now, the man on the wrong end of the gun fumbled at his right shirt pocket, brought out a small leather drawstring poke and dropped it on to the counter, coins clinking. 'There's enough in there to pay for a full two months' supplies — can you afford to refuse it?'

O'Malley curled a lip. 'I don't care if it's a flour sack full of double eagles — it won't buy *you* one thing here, mister.'

The tall man, in his early twenties, gave O'Malley — and the shotgun — one more steady look, then nodded. 'You're right. I got better things to do than argue with a knothead like you.'

'Don't come back.'

'It'll be hard to resist your hospitality.'

'Close that damn door after you!'

The lock clicked solidly behind the rejected customer. O'Malley put the shotgun away, then jumped as a man of mid-height wearing a buff-coloured narrow-brimmed hat stepped out from behind the shelves displaying smokers' requirements.

'Judas! Where the hell'd you come from?'

The man, in his early forties and dressed well in frock coat and flowered vest, brown pin-striped trousers, smiled thinly, a neat moustache along his upper lip reacting to the movement. 'Sorry, friend, was looking for some pipe tobacco back there but couldn't see my brand anywhere.'

'Which one is it?'

'Indian Head, I — '

'Won't find that in my store! I don't have no truck with Injuns in any shape or form. Can let you have some Republican, Royal Albert, Southern Way or — '

'No. I favour Indian Head. I'll try somewhere else.'

The voice was firm and brown eyes looked straight into O'Malley's watery red ones. 'How did you know that young feller was an ex-jailbird?'

O'Malley's jaw jutted a little more. 'I know who he is,' O'Malley said, flatly, deciding not to push this stranger. 'He was mixed up with that bunch held up

26

the Wells Fargo Depot in August Creek, a while back. Caught helpin' Morgan hisself.'

The other was interested now. 'Mmm, yes, I remember that. The gang killed all the Wells Fargo guards — '

'Includin' my brother! The sons of bitches!'

'And this fellow who was in here? I mean, the way I understood it, the posses were ruthless, killed every one of the robbers, brought them all in dead except the leader, Morgan, who got away for a time, but he paid the ultimate penalty, too, in the end.'

'Yeah, killed him in that kid's cabin up on the mesa. Dunno just what his part was, but when the posse nailed Morgan hisself on the kid's spread they reckoned he'd helped doctor his wounds and so on. And they wanted to know where the Wells Fargo satchel was Morgan was carryin', but the kid claimed Ace didn't have it with him at the cabin. Wouldn't change his story. They give him a few years in Yuma to think about it.' O'Malley shook his head jerkily. 'But he never told it any different.'

'Never revealed where the money was hidden?'

'Nah!' O'Malley bared yellowed teeth. 'Wells Fargo've still got a re-ward out for its recovery. Folk near tore the kid's spread apart up on the mesa while he was in Yuma but no one seen hide nor hair of it.'

'Bad luck.'

'God*damn* bad luck! I end up here in this man-an'-a-dog dump when I coulda had a store with my own manager runnin' it while I found me a woman to give me my comforts up there.' He jerked a thumb vaguely to the north. 'An' I'm talkin' about Chicago Heights society. There woulda been enough reward money to buy my way in.'

'Well, I'd best be going.'

'Close that door tight after you. Damn rannies come in and leave it ajar and store's full of grit and boot dung . . . an' half the time they don't even buy a thing!'

Opening the door, the frock-coated man smiled. 'Mind if I tell you something, friend?'

'What's that?' O'Malley was leery now.

'You're still a long, long way from Chicago Heights whether you have a valise full of money, or not. Good day to you.'

'Shut that goddamn door!'

*   *   *

From the shaded veranda of the store, the well-dressed man paused to look for the telegraph office, saw it across the street and down half a block.

There he sent a wire to a Mr Willard Moreno in Beaumont, Kansas. A very short wire, only two words: HE'S BACK. Plus the sender's name: CALDWELL.

The thin, tired-looking operator sent it and the man in the frock coat asked, 'How long before I can expect a reply?'

The operator yawned. 'You know your man better'n me, mister; up to

29

him, ain't it? He could answer right away or next Tuesday week . . . ' *For all I care*, he added under his breath.

'Mind if I wait?'

'This is an operatin' telegraph station, mister, no hotel waitin'-lounge. But there's one of them right across the street, even has waiters to bring you a drink.'

So Caldwell waited no more than two hours in the cool comfort of the foyer of the Keystone Palace Hotel before he received a reply from Mr Willard Moreno, a very brief reply: MAKE OFFER.

Caldwell smiled slowly, stopped a waiter and ordered another whiskey, then called the man back.

'No, make that a double, will you?'

It was worth an extra drink. Yes *sir!*

* * *

He was lucky he left the foyer when he did, just in time to see the young man who'd been in O'Malley's loading some sacks and a couple of small crates into the back of a battered and obviously much-repaired buckboard. *He'd found someone unbiased enough to serve him, it seemed . . .*

He was down by the only other general store in Keystone, not far from the livery barn. In fact, you could smell the hay and occasional stale urine from inside the store if the wind was just right.

Ross McCall was preparing to swing up into the driving seat when Caldwell hurried across, lifting an arm, calling, 'I say! I say, there!'

McCall glanced over his shoulder, still swinging aboard, and dropped on to the hard seat. He leaned forward swiftly and when he sat back again he had a rifle across his knees.

'You speakin' to me?' A neutral but wary tone.

Caldwell slowed his pace at sight of the gun, but managed a friendly smile as he came alongside the buckboard.

'I am indeed, if your name is Ross McCall. Oh, it is? Fine! I'm Virgil Caldwell, full-time attorney-at-law with a new office here in Keystone — thanks to the fruits of a most successful fraud case — '

'I don't need a lawyer.'

'I didn't mean to suggest you did, just introducing myself.'

He only received a quizzical stare in return.

'Er — yes, well, one of my clients may be known to you: Mr Willard Moreno, currently on a business visit to Beaumont, Kansas.'

'Never heard of him.' The man continued that steady stare and his answer was flat, final.

Caldwell smiled. 'Well, I believe he may well have expected you to say that, but he has asked me to put a proposition to you.'

'Ain't interested.'

'Oh, now, be reasonable! At least listen to what I have to say!'

'I can't think of a single reason why I would be interested in anything you have to say, on behalf of this . . . Moreno or anyone else.'

'If I could just explain — ?'

'Mister, *I just ain't interested!*' He emphasized the words and swung the rifle across, his thumb notching the hammer to half-cock.

Caldwell was sufficiently startled to take a step backwards. 'Wait up, there! No . . . no call for this!'

'You're right, and if you just step back a little more, I'll try to angle this here buckboard out without running over your feet . . . cripple you for life if that happened.'

Caldwell jumped backwards but the buckboard still swung perilously close as the driver slapped the reins across the backs of the two-horse team, gave a medium-loud, *Eeee-yaaaah!* and set the vehicle moving.

Licking his lips, Virgil Caldwell ran a few steps. 'Might I call on you up on Keystone Peak?'

'Try it and see.'

Caldwell didn't like the inference in those few flatly spoken words.

It sounded almost like a challenge.

3

The Offer

Virgil Caldwell waited a full day before he hired a horse well used to riders who preferred to travel at a sedate pace.

The liveryman didn't seem eager to talk, though he was polite enough when he did.

'Just you let him set the pace,' he advised, 'an' you won't have no trouble. Try usin' spurs or cuffin' him across the ear — well, I'd send a man after you if you weren't in by sundown.'

'That's very encouraging,' Caldwell said with a bit of snap in his tone. 'I want to ride up Keystone Peak — is that too adventurous for this animal?'

'Dunno why you'd want to go up there, but, hell, no, he'll make it all right. Got lotsa stamina.' The liveryman squinted. 'Only one man I know of lives up there.'

'That's the one I want to see: Ross McCall.'

The liveryman paused, then said, 'Sundown's still your deadline or it's another day's hire.'

'You know this McCall?'

'Nope. Heard a lotta gossip but paid no attention to it. Far as I know he treats hosses well and that's a plus in my book. Now, I was you, I'd get goin', you got quite a ways to ride.'

'Yes, I'll take your advice, but first, do you have any workers? Roustabouts would do as long as they were trustworthy.'

'I got one permanent man and a coupla fellers come in when I get busy; why?'

Caldwell looked around. 'I don't see anyone.'

''Cause I ain't *busy!* Now what you want?'

'Perhaps I could talk with one of your . . . sometime workers? One who might like to earn an easy dollar or two?'

'Hell, you won't need to hire a guide

to the mesa! Look, you can see it from here.' The stableman paused when he saw impatience on Caldwell's face. 'Link Taggart can always use an extra buck, but he's a mite unsociable.'

Caldwell smiled thinly. 'Ah! Can you fetch him?'

★ ★ ★

Caldwell was pleasantly surprised to find the hired mount very obedient to his signals and, apart from it insisting on a stop at Elbow Creek for a drink, standing belly-deep to cool down while doing so, there was little time lost.

The climb was easier than he expected, but the trail went all the way to the top where he found an old line camp building obviously being patched up. It looked as if a windstorm had wrecked it. He had the thought — accurately, as it turned out — that this was an abandoned line camp from one of the now-departed ranches that had tried unsuccessfully to work this mesa and its mediocre pastures. The word was you could buy one of those abandoned cabins for a few dollars, or take a chance and just move in.

He recognized the battered buck-board he had seen in town and saw half-a-dozen horses in a corral at the rear of the building. There was a small, barn-like structure where McCall probably kept his saddle gear and tools, but no sign of the man himself. Cattle bawled in some close-by but unseen pasture.

Caldwell walked his tired mount to a well under a shady tree, lowered the pail way down into water he couldn't see, and sweated it back up. He was sipping his second dipperful when he heard a sound that made his skin prickle: a rifle lever jacking a cartridge into the breech.

He froze, stomach leaping a little. 'I'm very thirsty, I didn't see anyone around.'

'Turn around — slow — and that'll change.'

Caldwell, lowering the dipper now,

turned and put on a smile. 'We meet again and, after all, you did sort of invite me.'

Ross McCall, still wearing the crudely patched clothes of earlier, smiled coldly, his rifle cocked and holding steadily on Caldwell. 'Water your horse — now.'

Caldwell grabbed the pail, slopping water as he hurriedly set it down off the well edge where the town horse could reach it. 'Horses come first up here,' McCall told him.

The attorney nodded jerkily, listened briefly to the horse slurping, then said, 'You know, I asked could I call on you and you said, I believe, 'Try it and see.' Well, here I am. I hope you'll make me welcome.'

'I don't like visitors. Got too much damn work to do.'

'Then you should've made that very clear, young man. I've gone to a great deal of trouble to get here and some little expense.'

'Yeah. You hired one of Lasky's mounts and, if I ain't mistaken, Link

Taggart.' He raised his voice. 'That you, Link? Skulkin' behind them big rocks? I seen you twenty minutes back; had an idea you might've been the advance war party.'

'Oh, come now, you exaggerate! This is no *war party*! I have come here on behalf of my principal, Mr Willard Moreno.'

'Still dunno him nor wish to.'

Caldwell's smile widened; he saw that Ross McCall had most of his attention concentrated on the rocks where Link Taggart still hadn't shown himself.

'Well, he's a rich man, very influential. Might be useful in setting you on a smoother path and a more profitable one. *Very* profitable I may add.'

'Link! You gonna come out, or do I have to make you?'

Hard on the last word, McCall lifted the rifle to his shoulder and put two bullets into the clump of rocks, the lead screaming away, sending a flock of birds screeching from the treetops.

Caldwell jumped and felt the sweat

bead his forehead and trickle down from his armpits. *He hadn't expected this!* Or perhaps he had, subconsciously, which was why he had hired Taggart, although it looked as if that money may have been ill-spent.

But wait! *No!* By heaven, Taggart had shown more intelligence than the liveryman had allowed for: he had brought a sidekick of his own. As Taggart, big and shambling with the red, watery eyes and blue-veined nose of the heavy drinker, showed himself, arms raised, a second man Caldwell had seen briefly in the livery appeared at the tree-line just down the slope.

He was lean as a rail, hook-nosed, and looked kind of frail, but this was off-set by the double-barrelled shotgun he held.

The loud *click* of the hammer cocking froze Ross McCall, who turned his head slowly. 'Should've realized your boozin' pard wouldn't be far away, Link. Howdy, Harp. Guess you want me to put down my rifle?'

'You better!' croaked the lean man lifting the shotgun menacingly as Link Taggart came forward, chuckling.

'OK. No need for anyone to get excited.' McCall held the rifle out to one side as Link came up, mouth curling now as he reached for the weapon.

He took it — across the side of his head as the ex-convict moved so fast Caldwell later swore the rifle barrel actually blurred before it almost swiped Taggart's head off. And a second later, even before Taggart had sprawled on the slope, McCall fired a bullet between Harp's spread boots. The man danced wildly, pulling his triggers. The shotgun roared and leapt from his grip as he pranced an impromptu jig. He sprawled, and managed to snatch up the smoking shotgun again, rising swiftly and striking at McCall's legs with the long, heavy barrels. The younger man leapt back, missed his footing and stumbled. Harp, on his feet now, swung the shotgun at his head, but McCall twisted violently, grabbed the weapon and yanked hard.

Harp staggered in against him and screamed as a knee rammed into his crotch. Grabbing at himself, moaning sickly, he fell and writhed on the slope.

Caldwell seemed frozen where he stood. Then abruptly lifted his hands shoulder-high.

'It seems I underestimated you, sir! My apologies! I did not expect to use these — fools — in this manner, merely as back-up, but I can see now you would not have been intimidated.'

'Neither by them nor you, Counsellor!' The prison-sound was strong in McCall's voice now. 'Told you I don't know this Moreno, don't want to know him. An' I'm tired of lookin' at you!'

Caldwell was sweating freely now, licked his dry lips and moved sideways across the slope a few feet.

'I . . . I have made a *genuinely* bad mistake, sir! I offer my apologies again. Just look at these idiots! Would you believe they cost me twenty dollars?'

'Makes you the idiot.'

Caldwell managed a glare. 'Perhaps.

But as I'm here — '

'You're already on your way down the slope. Just follow those clowns you brought with you.'

He pointed to the limping, stumbling pair, helping each other, slipping and sliding down the slope.

'As I am *here*,' Caldwell managed again, his insides knotting up now, 'please allow me to make Mr Moreno's offer. I — I'm sure — '

'Mister, you are one boneheaded sonofabitch. I think I might even bend my rifle barrel a little more on your thick skull!'

'Waitwaitwait!' Caldwell's hands were stretched out at full length as if pushing away some terror confronting him. He cringed as the rifle came up but McCall held off using it.

Caldwell took his chance and yelled, 'He'll give you a thousand dollars just for listening to the offer, another thousand if you agree to take it and a whopping — '

By now the rifle muzzle was pushing

hard into Caldwell's soft midriff and he sounded as if he were choking as he swallowed further words. His eyes were actually bulging.

'Those fools you brought have a head-start on you. Get going and see if you can catch 'em up, Counsellor.'

Caldwell began backing away towards his mount, looking warily over his shoulder.

'May I tell Mr Moreno you are . . . considering . . . his offer?'

'Judas priest, man! You're not only persistent, you're plain damn loco! Now get the hell outa here!'

The rifle fired and Caldwell screamed as a bullet burned across his outer left thigh, ripping out a trouser pocket, coins scattering across the slope. He gasped, clasping his burning hip as fear pulsed through him like heatwaves from desert rock.

'Go!' McCall said surprisingly quietly — and clearly. 'I could've broken your hip just now. I even *see* you again near here, I'll shoot to kill.'

Caldwell was making all kinds of wild signs with his hands as he fumbled to climb aboard his mount. He managed it, ungainly but successfully. As he lifted the reins and started downslope, he found a little courage hiding somewhere deep inside him and said quite forcefully and bitterly, 'I think you are going to be very sorry, McCall! Very sorry!'

'Not as sorry as you if I see you up here again. Or anyone else claims to come from this damned Moreno.' He fired the rifle into the air. 'Now git!'

Caldwell wasted no time in obeying.

* * *

The telegraph operator signed off from the message that had just rattled in on his key, picked up the paper where he had written down the words and looked narrowly across the counter to where Caldwell stood.

He was composed and dressed perfectly in his usual frock-coat and vest outfit now. No one would believe that he had gone through such trauma only hours earlier on the darkening slopes of that mesa. The attorney had stopped only to clean up and bandage his bullet-burned thigh wound. Looking as dapper and confident as ever, he had wasted no more time in sending his report to Mr Moreno, which had been very brief: OFFER REFUSED. Now he reached for the paper the operator pushed at him.

'You ain't exactly addin' to the profits of this office, mister. One- and two-word messages! Hardly worthwhile rattlin' my key.'

The man stopped speaking as he saw Caldwell scan the message. This one was just as succinct as the earlier ones.

All it said was: WAIT.

As the operator continued his complaints, the key began rattling again and he swivelled his chair round swiftly, clicked his personal on-line acknowledgement and started to smile across at Caldwell.

'He's runnin' off at the mouth this time!'

Caldwell waited curiously but it seemed only seconds before the man signed off, scanned his message slip, then handed it across.

'Musta had an attack of verbal diarrhoea,' he commented.

The message was longer than Caldwell had sent — or received — for a long time when in contact with the distant Moreno.

MEET CAPROCK STAGE KEY-STONE TOMORROW NOON STOP MR CONNOR WILL MAKE HIMSELF KNOWN STOP YOU WILL FIND HIM MOST EFFICIENT STOP WM

'You know,' the operator said with a touch of a whine, 'you're supposed to sign a wire with your full name. This WM, I guess, is the Moreno you been contactin' — must have some clout if they OK'd his wire with only initials.'

'He has tremendous clout as you call

47

it. I'd remember that if you were thinking of talking about this aspect — or any other — of the wires I have received or sent recently.'

'Christ! One-worders! What the hell you think I could give away with lousy one-worders?'

Caldwell smiled smugly. 'How about your life?' He paused at the door. 'Worth thinking about . . . ?'

4

Hardcase

'You're late.'

Virgil Caldwell smiled as he shook his head slowly, gesturing to the bustling crowds at the stage depot.

'No, the stage is early.'

'Which makes you late.'

Caldwell's smile slowly disappeared as he looked into the clean-shaven, lean-jawed face of this man with the piercing black eyes, his features shaded by the brim of his fore-and-aft crowned hat. He was a tall man, about thirty, a tuft of hair showing at the open neck of his red shirt as he shouldered his warbag. His clothes were a standard range outfit of fair quality, just tight enough to show he was well muscled. He carried a sheathed rifle in his other hand, using his elbow to hitch back the walnut-handled Colt he wore on his hip.

Caldwell gestured to the buckboard, standing in the shade of the adobe building.

'Soon as you can, get me a good mount,' Connor said, heaving his gear into the buckboard's tray. 'And I mean *good*.'

'The livery has a fair selection you can look over at your leisure, after we get you booked into the hotel.'

Connor stopped, suddenly blocking the attorney as Caldwell made for the driving seat. He looked steadily into the startled man's face.

'Caldwell, I said *you* get me a good mount and do it soon. I've got a tight agenda.'

'Well, I have a business to run, and — ' Caldwell swallowed the rest of his words as the rifle muzzle jarred under his ribcage, pushing him back a couple of involuntary steps. He made a small squeaking sound.

'Didn't Mr Moreno make it clear to

you, you damned dude? *I'm here to do what has to be done*, which takes time to plan. You take care of my wants so I can get on with it — you savvy that?'

Caldwell's face was flushed and his heart was hammering as he nodded vigorously. 'I-I didn't quite understand just what your position was — '

'I'm Señor Moreno's trouble shooter. Now you know. Let's move.'

He half expected Connor to complain or be pernickety about the accommodation but the man barely glanced at the hotel room, tossed his dusty, worn bags on the bed and pointed to the door as he lay down beside them — spur rowels digging into the coverlet. 'I'm tired — gonna take a nap. When I wake up I expect to find directions to this McCall's place and a damned good description or map. OK?'

The attorney drew himself up and there was a slight tremor in his voice as he said, 'Now, listen here, my man, I didn't expect treatment such as this and I'm sure Mr Moreno will instruct you to be more . . . polite and co-operative when I advise him of your — *Aaah!*'

This last burst from Caldwell as the six-gun appeared in Connor's gloved right hand, the hammer cocked. As the man sat up effortlessly on the bed, the blade foresight came into contact with the attorney's flabby cheek. It dug deep as Connor applied pressure, the metal almost buried in the soft flesh.

'Will you, for Chris'sake, *shut up*, and let me get some shuteye? Or I swear I'll mark you for life, jawbone to hairline!'

Caldwell grabbed the bedpost to momentarily steady his suddenly weak legs, swallowed and then nodded. 'I-I'll see to whatever you want, Mr Connor. Horse, map, I'll arrange a canteen of fresh water for your saddle and a grub sack — '

'Don't just talk about it, get it done.'

Caldwell made for the door, sweating, his bladder beginning to burn as it urgently signalled it needed voiding.

Connor sat up on the bed, holding

the six-gun until the door closed behind the other. Then he grunted and lay down again.

He was asleep in minutes, the gun still clasped in his right hand.

Outside, and halfway down the stairs to the hotel foyer, Caldwell paused to mop his face with an initialled kerchief, glanced back at the closed door of room Number 7 and muttered, 'Damned hardcase!'

But he didn't say it too loud . . .

★ ★ ★

The man known as Ross McCall worked hard, stripped to the waist, sweating, taking the odd tool cut or bruise from mishandled timber but ignoring it: his wounds could be treated after he had finished work for the day.

The place had been in one hell of a mess when he'd arrived back from Yuma. He had smiled wryly as he looked at the pile of timber, exposed building frames, a roof nearly devoid of

53

shingles. 'Bet you didn't find it, boys,' he said softly. 'That's all that kept you from burnin' me out completely, I reckon, just in case you had missed it in your search.' He sobered a little, then, 'If you haven't found that damn satchel by now, I dunno what chance I have.'

He knew he was in for a time of it, putting the place back together. Luckily he enjoyed carpentry and he'd been able to polish his skills at it in Yuma, even if his efforts were usually rewarded with cuffs and kicks or a cane across the shoulders.

But he was doing a pretty good job of repairing the old line cabin, had even dragged a few riverstones up the slope — the effort almost killed him — and cemented them in around the base.

He cut shingles of fair quality from what timber was available, felled usable trees, ate only one meal a day and went to bed at the same time as the birds.

Several times, he was awake before them, amusing himself by imitating their morning calls as he washed in the creek. He worked with old tools, likely left behind by the ranch crew when they abandoned the place, often had to stop to repair or sharpen them. Anyone watching — and there were some — had to admit he seemed to know what he was doing.

Up in the rocks near the very top of the peak, Lee Connor squatted in a shady place he had made for himself, watched through a pair of army field-glasses, actually admiring Ross's work.

'Nothin' like a good old stretch of jail hard labour to teach a man how to build things,' he told himself. 'Them guards know when to enforce an idea with their billies or whips. Reckon you had you a few lessons, feller.'

There were raised criss-crossed scars on McCall's back that rippled with the movement of his muscles, drawing attention to them. They were thicker than the original ones and there were more of them . . . which said something about McCall's stay in Yuma. *No bed of roses . . .*

'You musta been a baaad boy, or a

dumb one, feller. I'm thinkin' baaad, 'cause you're making a real nice job of this place. Give you another week and I reckon you'll be ready to start on the inside . . . '

★   ★   ★

'*Another* week!' echoed Virgil Caldwell, looking up at Connor sitting on the other side of his desk, making himself comfortable in a padded chair. 'Man, you have been here twelve days! And I've already had two very terse wires from Mr Moreno! He wants some action.'

'And he'll get it when I'm ready.' Connor took out a cheroot and lit it.

'Well, for heaven's sake, when will that be?'

'I'll let you know.'

'But Mr Moreno was expecting — '

'Señor Goddamn Moreno will get just what he's expecting, and more. In — my — good — time!'

Caldwell shook his head, wrote for a

few minutes, hoping Connor would leave, but the man seemed content where he was.

'I — er — don't know much about your duties, Mr Connor, but it seems to me that you — er — *should* have produced something by now. Mr Moreno wants this McCall to fully understand that his refusal to even listen to his proposition is not acceptable.'

'Oh, McCall'll get the message all right — loud and clear.'

Caldwell leaned forward. 'When?'

Connor surprised him by smiling. 'How does tonight sound?'

* * *

Ross McCall was pretty much exhausted when he turned in with the birds, because he couldn't stay awake any longer, gave in and tumbled down into a deep, dreamless sleep.

It had been a long chore, restoring this old line camp: the men who had abandoned it had let it go to rack and ruin, not caring, because their boss was ailing, and the foreman had helped himself to a lot of gear that would bring a good price — then vamoosed.

The crew had stripped the place of what they figured they could sell and also vamoosed. Some of them had taken delight in kicking in wall panels and cupboards, busting up the window shutters and betting on how many kicks it would take to tear the main door off its hinges.

McCall had thought if ever he caught up with some of those destructive sons of bitches they would be the ones who'd need repairing.

It had been a challenge, bringing the building back to liveable condition — and adding to it here and there. Two extra cupboards along an empty wall, a couple of decent chairs to go with the newly strengthened table, renewing the planked floor in front of the wood range, adding a wall flap that would allow him to poke gathered kindling and small logs through from outside.

And a new bunk. He had other plans but, for now, it was ready for occupation and he was looking forward to laying in some stores and building a zigzag chute of lodgepole leading down to the corral he had thrown up in amongst some brush so it wouldn't be seen by the running mavericks or mustangs until it was too late to turn away. Yeah, it would be good to run both cattle and horses.

It would be mighty hard work rounding up the high-country mustangs, though, but he knew he could handle it — and the body-jarring breaking-in afterward? We-ell, he *had* to do it, that was all there was to it.

The man who had tried to raise cattle here had been an amateur: there was adequate grass, but it was in patches between trees rugged enough to grow hardy and surprisingly tall. Sure, the cows would eat where they could, but they preferred the fields where they could wander, bellow at the hot blue dome of the sky and chew cud

— enjoying the view, for all he knew! But he'd clear a dozen or so trees, give 'em shoulder room, and aimed to try both cattle and horses, sure he could make a go of it.

The original owner had taken ill and had grown stubborn and stupid and had refused to listen to men who knew better. The place was abandoned and vandalized right under his nose by a crew who hadn't been paid in months: that made McCall wonder why they'd stayed put. Likely had some lucrative deal going with the shadowy men who slipped back and forth across the border, which wasn't all that far away.

Time dragged by in Yuma and eventually, surprised that he had survived his unnecessary sentence, Ross McCall had been released and here he was in the only place on earth that he could claim belonged to him.

Luckily he had had a few dollars left him by his father in the bank and it had gathered some welcome interest while he did jail-time.

He was willing — *eager* — to bust a gut and bring this line camp up to a liveable condition. With just a little more work, he would be ready to move in and build some kind of future for himself.

Ready — steady — *go!*

The trouble was, Lee Connor figured different.

5

'Get the Message?'

It was always hot in the cabin, even on top of this mesa, and McCall had planned some extra ventilation for future summers.

But this night it seemed inordinately hot, making him toss and turn, lying on top of the bunk's meagre sheets and blankets. Half-awake, he sat up and tore off the old shirt he slept in, but he was still beaded with sweat and even found it harder to breathe.

And why wouldn't he? The cabin was full of smoke, thickening by the minute!

He rolled off the bunk, bare feet automatically feeling for his boots. He hopped on one foot then the other as he forced the boots on, shaking his head, eyes beginning to sting.

Then he saw the flames.

Not just in one place, but all along the base of the walls — and the big door.

He knew what that meant!

The fire had been deliberately lit and it was a good bet he wasn't meant to get out alive! Or maybe he was, but only after having seven kinds of hell scared out of him. Well, they'd made a good start there!

Instinct took over. Before he realized it, he was buckling on his six-gun rig, had grabbed the fringed buckskin sheath containing his rifle, with the bullet loops riveted on the outside, holding a dozen extra cartridges, over and above what was already in the magazine.

There was no glass to worry about: he picked up the new chair he had made and splintered it as he bashed and rammed at the shutter nearest the rear of the cabin: it had been jammed shut with a wedge of green timber on the outside.

Then there was a rushing sound overhead and he looked up in time to see naked flames stabbing through the unlined shingle roof. Half-a-dozen flaming shingles rained down on him from several directions and he lifted his arms to shield himself as he stumbled and sprawled full length. But he maintained his grip on the rifle, rolled away from the falling shingles and twisted up to his knees.

The walls now were blazing — the stench of coal oil thick and heavy in his flared nostrils. Well, he didn't need that to confirm his first thoughts about an arsonist, but it spurred him to that window shutter again. He wrenched up one of the thick planks from the section he had laid in front of the old stove.

Smoke was choking him, stinging his eyes, filling his lungs with rasping, raw heat, gripping his throat like a hostile fist.

Whoever had done this had worked professionally: he hadn't been aware of anything until the smoke had rasped his nostrils. *Lady Luck was with him so far.*

The plank was heavy and, being short

of air to start with, he dropped it twice before he gave a roar he didn't realize he had enough breath for and ran at the shutter. The plank hit like a battering ram, splintered the horizontal wood strips — and jammed.

He twisted as he felt flames at his back, searing his neck, and he briefly wondered about his long, unkempt hair. His hands were hot and he realized the plank he held was burning now, began to release it, but bared his teeth, grappled it over a section with only small flames and made another run at the window shutter. This time it splintered the whole panel and it fell away to one side — he didn't bother to check which. Instead, he snatched up his rifle, had to jerk it from the leather scabbard that was enveloped in flames now and dived headlong out into the night — even as the spare cartridges he had fixed to the scabbard started to pop in a staccato volley, lead buzzing and whining about like a swarm of mad bees.

Then he was out of the cabin, rolling away, half scrabbling across the gravel which raked one side of his face and head and tore at his hands.

But he was *out* and that was the main thing.

He ran to the nearest rock, found it too hot, slid and skidded to the next group and, gasping, coughing, feeling as if he was about to spit up a lung, leaned against the granite, blinking as he watched what had been his future only minutes ago, turning the night into flickering day . . .

What was left of the roof suddenly caved in, sending burning shingles high into the air like shooting stars.

He swore and cussed like he never had before but abruptly bit off an epithet, standing there impotently with clenched fists.

Come on! *Worry about who did it afterwards: just get the hell out of here — right now! Save your neck!*

The creek was slightly uphill but he only had a couple of pails and — He grabbed a pick and desiccated earth flew from under the driving blade. A small trickle of water started but he quickly realized he wasn't going to be able to dig a trench deep enough to allow a worthwhile volume of water to pour down to the fire.

Blowing hard, resting on the pick handle for a moment, he watched the past few months of killing work being destroyed in front of his stinging eyes. He flung the pick aside and ran back towards the burning framework of the cabin, having to hold his hands in front of his face against the heat and roiling smoke.

Then he paused, only feet from the burning door. *What the hell was he doing? There wasn't a damn thing in there that was worth risking his life for!*

One thing prison taught a man: he had to make hard decisions quickly because he knew deep down there was no alternative. Like now: go back in there for — what? Nothing he needed. *He had his weapons: he wouldn't go hungry. Bedding? That was a laugh. He'd lived through a couple of truly freezing winters in Yuma with nothing but corn-sacks for cover.* No, there was little he could do except stand and watch the destruction.

The fire was going to raze his cabin and 'there was nothing he could do about it. Goddammit! What he'd hoped would be his *home!* — and he'd be left with nothing but a pile of blackened ashes and the rags he stood in.

The flames had already spread to the young trees he had allowed to grow close to the cabin for protection from the high country winds and maybe other kinds of dangers. Luckily he had had the forethought to clear the natural firebreaks down below the treeline, too — he hadn't wanted the whole damn mesa to burn should fire ever threaten. There were ranches down there. So: save himself, that was all he could do and, if he managed that, *then* go look for the sonofabitch who had set this fire!

Moving into the rocks again for protection from the heat, seeing much of the mountain lit up by the spreading, roaring, leaping flames, he thought about 'who?' It could be anybody. He wasn't popular in Keystone, neither town nor the whole blamed county, but mostly folk let him be. Early on there had been a time when he had been forced to fight someone whenever he went to town. And there'd been plenty of refusals to serve him in the stores — O'Malley was a latecomer in that field. But he wouldn't bend to their bullying.

Then the sheriff, Rafe Fuller, a tough old *hombre*, had made it clear that McCall had served his time and been legally released as a free man. He had a right to be given his chance to earn a place in society again.

'But why *our* society?' someone shouted.

Fuller had merely shrugged. 'That's the way it is. Give him a chance. I see it ain't workin' and I'll send him on his way.'

Many of the townspeople doubted

that, but the tough old sheriff was still a force to be reckoned with and, despite all the bitching and intolerance, McCall had stayed, on his mesa, and got on with the job of rebuilding the old line camp.

And now all he could do was watch as his efforts went up in smoke. In fact, he couldn't even do that. The flames had really taken hold in the timber now and it must look like a giant beacon from down in the town or from any trail leading there, as the entire top of the mesa went up in flames, the heat and glare driving him back.

Still no one came to help. But he freed his few cows, let them run; rounding them up again wouldn't take long, but he might just let them roam — looking for feed.

He saw the groups gathered below, many in night attire, some with hastily flung-on clothes, a few mounted, all staring up at the burning mesa. No doubt some were enjoying the sight. Maybe most . . .

At least one of them would be laughing inwardly at the chaos and damage he had caused.

For a while, maybe — only for a while, feller!

* * *

There was still plenty of smoke come sun up, the air hazy and pungent, the stink irritating, unavoidable.

A couple of dozen townsfolk were still at the foot of the mesa, now blackened for almost halfway down the slopes. They were mostly men, staring, some using field-glasses to examine the site of the fire.

'Wonder if the sonofa'll get the message?' someone asked.

'He's gotta be dumber'n a drunken squaw if he don't.'

'You ask me, McCall ought to think about moving out, pronto — if he's got any sense.'

All heads turned to the speaker. The comment was made by Lee Connor, neatly dressed for this early in the morning and in such a place.

'Why you say that?'

'Hell! Would you stay? I mean, whoever done it obviously waited until he'd just about finished his rebuildin', all ready to move in!' He chuckled. 'That's what I call real mean.'

'Mean, all right!'

'Friend, only an idiot would hesitate to move out after someone did that . . . I mean, that message says, clear as daylight to me, *Git! And right now!*'

The others thought about it briefly and then nodded agreement. 'Yeah! *Git!* Or we'll set *your* ass on fire next!'

That brought a chuckle, but it sounded a little strained: Keystone wasn't a town used to this kind of trouble . . .

Connor added nothing more to the conversation and soon the group broke up, men going back to their homes: plenty to talk about in the course of this dawning day.

Connor smoked by a tree until they

were out of sight, then made his way to a small arroyo where he had left his horse. It was still skittish with the stink of smoke so strong, but he mounted and rode around the base of Keystone Peak, like a giant pimple on the mesa's tablctop.

Then he put the mount up the slope and zigzagged his way up the mesa, stopping on a smouldering ridge. He paused, half rose in the saddle, so he could see past some blackened rocks, and sat back grinning.

Ross McCall was still down there on the bench where the cabin had stood, pawing over the charred remains, using a rake with a blackened handle and tines.

Connor set his mount down at an easy pace, getting in quite close before McCall heard him above the clatter of timber he was raking aside. Connor hauled rein sharply as a six-gun appeared in McCall's right hand, cocked.

Judas! That was fast!

'If you have notions of helpin' out,' McCall said coldly, 'you're too damn late. If you don't, keep ridin'.'

Connor lifted his hands halfway to his chest.

'Well, just wondered if there was somethin' I could help with, the cleanin'-up mebbe. Sure is a damn mess. Nothin' much you could salvage, I guess.'

'Nothing at all. And I ain't aimin' to clean up.'

'Movin' on?'

'Didn't say that. Who're you? You're not from around here.'

'No, just passin' through and — well, I heard some talk about you not being popular anywheres here and — well, I'm the kinda feller likes to see the one no one likes and try to figure out why.'

Connor smiled when he said it but Ross's soot-smeared, sober expression didn't change. 'If you know I ain't popular, then you know I'm an ex-jailbird.'

Connor nodded slowly: he hadn't expected candour right now. 'Well, you musta served your time, I guess.'

'Don't count around here. You look smart enough to've figured this out for yourself. What d'you really want?'

Connor thought for a long minute, scratched a little stubble beginning to show on his jaw. 'Fact is, I was wonderin' if you'd got any kinda message outa this?'

Ross stiffened, eyes narrowing. 'Message?'

Connor waved a languid hand. 'Has to be some kinda warnin', I reckon.'

'Warning? Man, more than that! They must figure by now they've left me no choice except to move on.' Connor's face had tightened some as McCall added, '*If* I move on, it'll be because I want to, not because some fool thinks a fire will scare me off.'

The hard eyes were boring into Connor, who was mildly surprised at the feeling of nervous pressure in his belly. *Not many men walking this earth could say they'd made Lee Connor jumpy, even for a minute.*

But this McCall —

It riled Connor that he had felt a shaft of fear, looking into this man's face. He grew reckless, said a little more than he meant to.

'If someone sent me a message as plain as this one, I'd blame well heed it! In case the next time was more serious.'

I'm different. Don't even know who's behind the damn thing — whatever his reason is.'

Connor thought for a moment, decided to use shock tactics. 'You're not wanted, that's what it says. Did hear there's someone named Reno or Moreno, somethin' like that, has an interest in you.'

McCall didn't move. The hard expression and clamped jaw showed no signs of relaxing. But, as Connor slowly dismounted, those eyes were suddenly like the tips of bullets showing in the cylinder of a pistol aimed at Connor's head. He cursed himself silently.

Damn! He'd let this ranny rattle him! Wanted to shake him up, but now he might've tipped his hand.

McCall said quietly, 'I don't know any Moreno or whoever, but mebbe you do.'

Connor hesitated: it was too late to back off now and, anyway, it was time McCall had something shoved right under his nose where he could see it . . . *and heed the warning*.

'I've — heard of him, yeah.'

A hard gaze steadied on Connor. 'Who the hell is he? And what's he want with me?'

Connor shrugged. 'He's no one to mess with, can tell you that much.'

Ross McCall looked mean and thoughtful now, spoke slowly. 'Told you to get my attention, did he?' he said, gesturing briefly to the cabin's remains.

'I didn't say I knew him that well!' Connor's recklessness in trying to shake up this ranny some was going down a track he hadn't meant it to. 'You get the idea, though.'

He said this last with a crooked smile, but next second that smile was wiped clean off his face by McCall's gun barrel that moved no more than eight inches and nearly took Connor's head off, sent him toppling, dazed and shocked.

'Now I'll give *you* a message for Mr Goddamn Moreno whoever the hell he is! *Just let me be!*' He moved in on the floundering Connor as the man tried to get up out of the dust. A hard boot bent the struggling man's ribs and sent him rolling down the slope into the edge of the smouldering ash. It was hot and he jumped up, swearing, swiping at his smoking sleeve. He kicked a shower of coals at McCall then two more hard blows snapped his head back.

He yelled, hands clawing at his face, half-doubling over. Before he could recover, a barrage of relentless, hammering blows raked his ribs and chest, squashed one ear, which stung like *hell*! Then Connor was crowded back and a boot like a kick from a horse took him in the middle of the chest and thrust him down beside a still-smoking length of what had once been a roof support.

Connor fumbled for his six-gun, found his hand pinned brutally by a scuffed, ash-covered boot. 'Like to play with fire, do you?' McCall asked, panting from his exertions. 'OK — see how you like this!'

As Connor struggled frantically, McCall clamped his hand over the man's temples and forced the side of his face against the glowing coals . . . just for a second, but it was enough to make Connor howl and buck and curse. Ross stepped back, fists cocked, allowed Connor to roll away, holding his burned and blistered face, almost sobbing.

'You — *bastard*.'

'You forgot, *amigo*, you're tangling with someone who spent years in the toughest jail in the country. You don't win fights in there: you survive 'em — if you're lucky. No quarter asked or given. You wanna beg off now?'

'I wanna *kill* you!'

McCall stood back and lifted his hands out from his sides. 'Stand up and we'll see if you can.'

Connor had never felt such a surge of fear mixed with humiliation. He was only glad there was no one to witness his plight. 'I'll get you, you sonofabitch!

I'll — get — you! When I'm good'n ready!'

'Better make sure it's what Moreno wants. He might prefer it if I stayed alive.'

Connor blinked: *now there was a thought, by God!* Moreno had never actually said one way or the other — *Wait!* He had!

' . . . I need Ross to do something for me that only he can do. Keep that in mind, but *bend him to breaking point — and maybe a little more if you can manage it. If you can't and you put on too much pressure . . .* '

The rest was left unspoken. Connor found himself in a sweat just thinking about that meeting with Moreno.

Christ! He was going to have to be mighty careful!

Who knew what Moreno had in mind? But his thoughts along those lines were quickly overwhelmed by the searing pain now surging through his entire head.

It seemed to reach his brain and, in

a second, he committed himself to a course of action he would remember for as long as he lived.

With a roar that echoed like a mountain lion in a cavern he suddenly propelled himself at McCall, catching the man off-guard. His sheer weight drove Ross to his knees and Connor beat and yelled, spittle flying, wild-eyed, as he hit out at his tormentor. All sounds were primitive, unintelligible: Connor had no idea what he was saying, only what he wanted — *had* — to do: and that was beat Ross McCall senseless.

McCall went down hard and glimpsed a worn boot heel driving at his face. He snapped his head aside and the heel gouged a trough above his ear. He jerked away as the boots stomped wildly, seeking any part of him.

At last he found a slope that allowed him to dig in his own heels and claw his fingers deep, thrusting desperately. He came up as if driven by some kind of powerful spring at the same time as Connor was leaning down towards him, reaching out for his throat.

They met with a bone-jarring thud that stopped both men in their tracks, winded, lights swirling before their eyes, brains feeling loose in their skulls.

Connor grunted and fell flat on his face. McCall spun away a few feet, contorted his aching body and grabbed at a rock. It was embedded firmly enough for him to use as a pivot. He came around on that rigid arm and dropped with both knees on to Connor's belly. The man gagged and coughed, but either by instinct or design, kept sliding and was suddenly diving between the other's spread legs.

He somersaulted, skidded to a halt, and by the time he whipped around, surprising himself at the security of his footing, McCall was still stumbling, trying to rise. Connor launched himself, grabbing a flat rock and lifting it, intending to smash his enemy's head in . . . and to hell with what Moreno wanted!

McCall read the intention and instinct took over. He slid left, then up, not down as might have been expected. The rock slammed into the ground where his head had been. He drove his boot in under Connor's raised arm, grinding deep.

Connor gasped sickly and stumbled, and a clenched fist like a hammer tumbled him away, violently. Disoriented, reaching out, but finding only thin air and no support, he began to slide, out of control.

McCall went after him, drew even, reaching for him, and Connor's left boot took him on the jaw. Stars swirled before he could recover, stumbling. Connor lurched upright and jumped, intending to land with both boots driving into McCall, whose hand was scrabbling for a grip that would give him purchase for an escape manoeuvre. He felt loose gravel, scooped up a handful and hurled it into Connor's face.

Instinctively, Connor's hands went up to protect his eyes in a lightning movement, leaving his body unprotected.

McCall planted his boots firmly,

hooked Connor just below the left ear, uppercut him with his other fist and swung again, but missed as Connor's body went past the point of balance. Barely conscious, Connor hit the slope, rolling, somersaulting, bouncing over low rocks, gathering speed, until he yelled loudly as he hurtled out of sight over a ledge.

Barely able to get a decent breath, McCall sat down heavily, fell on to his side, then flopped on to his back, chest heaving. His split knuckles were stinging and throbbing. His arms felt like lead and the sun was warm through the blood streaking his battered face.

He couldn't remember feeling so damn pooped since a long, long day on the rock pile. He flopped back and let the sun beat down on him as his heart gradually slowed.

His last thought before he passed out was: for his own safety he should finish off Moreno's man: that was the Yuma way. But, murder had never been anything he could live with easily.

Besides, he wanted to meet this Moreno and find out just what the hell he wanted — or expected — from the man named Ross McCall.

6

Dark Mesa

McCall moved stiffly. Every muscle and bone ached. It was a long time since he'd had a knock-down, drag-out brawl like the one with Lee Connor.

He'd staggered to the rim of the ledge where Connor had dropped over. The man was sprawled face down in some long grass, unmoving. He looked dead, but, after a while, McCall, trying to staunch the blood flow from his own wounds, saw one leg kick as ants crawled up Connor's trousers. An automatic reaction, but he was alive and, as if to prove it, moved his head slightly. The side of his face that showed was a mask of blood with raw skin dangling in several places.

Somehow, McCall managed to get to the creek, then plunged in, fully clothed

— if you could call the bloody rags he still wore 'clothes'. He sat there, struggling out of his tattered shirt, rolled it up and used it as a pillow on a rock to keep his head above water. Then he closed his eyes and let his arms dangle down at his sides as the soothing, chill water enveloped his body.

He even dozed a little — suddenly started, jerked half-upright as he heard a horse. It was coming from below, must have climbed the mesa's steep trail. He began to struggle up properly, stupid with fatigue and the agony of the beating he had taken. Why else would he have left his guns on the creek bank? Man, he felt like he was trying to walk over a series of bobbing kegs in a river. He fell awkwardly climbing out of the water, rolled on to his back briefly.

He smiled wryly as he wondered how Connor must feel — *a whole damn lot worse, he hoped!*

'My God, it's my day for discovering bodies of strange men, it seems!'

The woman's voice startled him and he blinked water from his eyes, resting on one elbow now. He shook his head to clear his vision some more, saw a woman about his own age in range shirt and denim trousers, sitting a pinto. Leaning forward, hands folded on the saddle horn, she stared down at him. 'Are you by any chance Mr Ross McCall?'

Her voice was pleasant enough and he seemed a long time answering because of the ache in his chest and throat, but he nodded. 'Who . . . who're you?'

The words were slurred and she pushed back her hat, which had a wider brim than was usual for a woman, revealing chestnut hair. The sunlight washed over a pleasant enough face and flickered off hazel eyes. Her full lips moved as she smiled.

'I'm Dana Cooke. I suppose you could call me a neighbour of yours.' He frowned, and his lips moved but she couldn't make out any words. She gestured over her shoulder, downslope. 'That's my ranch at the foot of the mesa. Circle Fifty-five — the Double Five, we call it.'

He was standing now, swaying, aware of his bedraggled appearance and the blood from his wounds spreading freely since it had been diluted by his immersion. 'I've seen your place from up here — long ways off. You run cows and some horses in that pasture close in against the mesa, don't you?'

'Mostly cattle. If you hadn't made that firebreak I could've lost that pasture, and my herd, when your place burned last night.'

He was shaking his head before she finished speaking. 'Well, that firebreak — it was a sort of accident. I was movin' some boulders when I first started clearing this site. A big one got away, smashed into a few others and started a small avalanche. The rolling rocks followed an old dried-out creek bed — you can still see traces of it. Flattened all the trees an' brush in the watercourse. It just looked like a natural firebreak to me, so I let it be.'

'But you cleared it later, made a proper break.'

'Well — yeah. I — er — almost set the mesa afire one time tryin' to make horseshoes on an open forge. It spread down as far as the break, which stopped it.'

'I know! I had all my men ready to ride up here and possibly throw you into the fire, because I thought it was going to destroy my pastures and herds.' She said it lightly enough but there was a serious look behind her eyes. 'You contained the blaze and made a first-class firebreak and — well, everyone said you were a loner, a dangerous man, best left alone. I was busy with branding and let it go at that. I don't usually listen to bigotry and I'm sorry I never made the effort to come and thank you before this.'

'Why should you be any different?' Even the roughness of his damaged throat couldn't cover his bitterness.

Her face was sober now and she gave him a brief, silent stare, before saying, 'You did serve your full sentence and then some, I believe. Paid your 'social debt' as they call it. I don't know why you aren't accepted in our town.'

He curled a lip. 'Ask your fellow citizens.'

The chestnut hair fell over her left eye as she nodded slowly. She pushed it back instinctively. 'Well, I suppose we're not the only town to show intolerance to ex-jailbirds — or the son of one — but —'

'The only one I've struck.'

'Oh! Be fair! You came here practically straight from Yuma, as I understand it! Eager to claim your — was it an inheritance, this place?' She gestured at the blackened ruins of his cabin.

'Kind of, I guess. The man who left it to me was close to my father. I don't know the full story. I was befriended by Ace Morgan after Pa was killed, and when that Wells Fargo thing went off the rails . . . ' He shrugged a little, wincing. 'Yeah, I helped him. Why wouldn't I? The man was wounded, a friend of my father's.' His voice dropped, then came back to a normal level. 'Guess I was lucky to get only a couple years in Yuma and not hang like some wanted. I was damn glad to have some place to come back to after I'd done my time.'

Her face took on a more kindly look. 'Yes, I — I think I can imagine how eager you must have felt.'

He shook his head. 'No, you can't.'

They looked at each other steadily and then she smiled. 'You're right. But I'm here at last and I am sorry I never made your acquaintance long before this.'

He couldn't quite cover the suspicion in his look. 'You said something about 'discovering bodies' when you first arrived?'

'Oh, yes! Coming up the trail I found a man lying in the long grass. He looked as if he'd fallen clear off a mountain top.' She allowed her voice to rise interrogatively and when he said nothing, added, 'I — I don't believe I've ever seen any man beaten so badly.'

He arched his blood-clotted eyebrows at her and gave a crooked smile as he held his arms slightly out from his sides, hands upturned. 'Well, standing before you . . .'

She couldn't help smiling. 'Till now, then,' she added and he even managed a half-laugh. 'My foreman took Mr Connor into town to the doctor — where I think you should go, too.' No response, so she said, 'I take it you and Connor don't see eye to eye?'

'That's one way of putting it.' He paused and gestured to the burned-out ruins. '*Mister* Connor's handiwork.'

'Oh, my God!' She straightened in the saddle and the pinto moved restively but quietened at a murmured command. 'I — Here I am, making light of this and — You really mean it? Connor deliberately burned your cabin?'

'No reason to doubt it.'

After a while she said, quietly, 'I

believe I can see now why it was such a brutal confrontation.' She paused, her face showing her disapproval. 'But it's done nothing to win over the citizens of Keystone as far as you're concerned. D'you realize that?'

He shrugged, winced as aches and pains stabbed through his shoulders. 'I don't give a damn about the people of Keystone. Most of the town came out to watch my place burn last night. No one offered to help save it, but they don't get rid of me that easy.'

'You're staying on just to spite the people of Keystone? Who probably had nothing to do with the fire?'

He stared back out of his blackened, piercing eyes.

'One reason.'

'I-I think you are a very stubborn man, Mr McCall.' When he said nothing, she added, 'And a foolish one.'

'Ma'am, I guess I'd better include you in the people I don't give a damn about, too.'

She shook her head slowly. 'I just

came to thank you for that firebreak. Something I should've done long ago, before it had to be put to the test, shall we say? Well, I've done it and, just to show you that all the folk of Keystone County are not like the pigheaded ones you've encountered so far, I'm offering to send up some of my crew to help you clear this mess away before you start rebuilding.' She looked at him severely. 'That is what you have in mind, I presume?'

'Right, but you don't owe me nothin'.'

'You're refusing my offer?'

'Well, I thank you for it, but you could've sent someone up when you saw the fire last night.'

She flushed. 'I — Yes, I could've, but I was worried about the safety of my herds. The fire was spooking them and I needed all my men on hand in case it jumped the firebreak, which hadn't been tested up till then.'

She let the words trail off: it was obvious he wasn't interested in her excuses. It made her angry, but she did her best to keep her voice more or less natural.

'I don't think they would've got here in time to be of much help, anyway. I think you would still have lost your cabin.'

'Likely so. But I'm in no hurry; I'll rebuild, however long it takes.'

'And risk someone burning your place down again?'

'That's the risk whether I do the rebuildin' or your men help out. Why get yourself in Dutch with this town? Specially for a stranger like me?'

'I'm not alone. What about Sheriff Fuller?'

'He says he's only doing his duty and, personally, he'd be happier if I moved on. He might put the clock on me any time.'

'Of course, you told him that moving on wasn't in your plans?'

He said nothing, battered face unrepentant.

She heaved a deep breath. 'My-oh-my! Whatever they did to you in that prison has put a chip on your shoulder as big as that boulder yonder!'

'Lucky I'm strong enough to carry it.'

'Oh, you are a very stubborn man, Mr McCall! I don't see how you can possibly fit in here or, more to the point, *why you would want to.*'

He actually smiled this time and put an index finger up across his puffed and cut lips.

'Yes! I don't doubt it is a secret! I just hope it doesn't get you killed! Or anyone else.'

No reply or obvious reaction. She suddenly looked around the area.

'You know, you've almost resurrected this mesa as it used to be: a huge, blackened tabletop rock. It was called Dark Mesa then.' She paused briefly, then told him, 'Long ago, when there was trouble with the Indians, there was a fierce fire here. It burned almost all the vegetation and left nothing but blackened soil and rocks. Someone nicknamed it Dark Mesa, but that name changed in time as the place revegetated and our town grew, and it became known simply as Keystone Peak to most folk. Though, it isn't really a peak at all, except for that northern rise, just a mostly flat tabletop mountain with a string of dead-end draws and small canyons. A rustler's paradise, my father used to say.'

'Well, it ain't now, and won't be, long as I'm here.' He said it challengingly and she frowned. There was something in his tone, and some glint in those eyes that made her feel he was on the defensive and maybe this had something to do with his stubbornness in wanting to stay.

Stay against rising odds that threatened to overwhelm him, *and real danger. After all, he could have died in that cabin fire. Was it courage or stubbornness?*

'Take my advice and see a doctor, Mr McCall,' she said, as she turned her patient pinto and started back down the slope. 'Good day to you.'

7

The Visitor

The rider who weaved his weary mount — a big grey carrying saddle-bags double the normal size — through a field of small boulders hauled on the reins and allowed the horse to blow for a few minutes.

He took off his hat, mopped his bearded face and then his thinning, steel-grey hair. When he set the hat back in place, he urged the mount forward and upward. It was obvious the grey was tired and reluctant, but it moved after a few more nudges with the spurless boot-heels. The man leaned forward and patted the sweating neck affectionately.

The grey gave a small snort that might have meant anything and continued on around a bend in the almost non-existent trail.

The rider shaded his eyes as he caught movement above, saw that there was a dark figure working at repairing what looked like a window frame — it was hard to tell with so much charred and half-burned timber lying about.

'Hey, there! Black man, where will I find Mr McCall?'

The figure looked up sharply. 'Y'all wantin' to see Boss McCall — *bawss?*'

'That is the worst accent I have ever heard! I assume *you* are McCall — and that black look is soot from the fire?'

White teeth flashed briefly against the filthy face. 'You got good eyes for an old man.'

'Not so old, though I admit to incipient rheumatism and a waning of — er — certain bodily functions, but I am Doctor Miles Sheehan, best but only sawbones in Keystone.'

McCall, heavily covered in soot from head to foot, climbed down from the framework he had been standing on. 'I'm about to wash up in the creek, Doc, but you've wasted your time if you figured to pick up any business.'

'Miss Dana Cooke thinks differently and asked me to look you up if I was over this way.'

'Which you are, but we'll talk soon.' McCall gestured to some bushes. 'Yonder, hidden by that bush, is the draw where I've built my lean-to which will serve until I can rebuild the cabin. You'll find coffee and a banked fire inside; see what kinda brew you can make while I become a white man again.'

'I'm not much of a hand *making* coffee. Drinking it, yes, I'm fine at that, but . . . '

McCall had already slid down the slope and plunged into the creek, sitting with water up to his waist, scrubbing at his skin with a handful of sand.

'You're rubbing far too hard! Too damn *hard* I say!' the medic warned. He paused and added in a slower voice, 'Careful you don't break those . . . welts on your back. My God! What a nest of them you have!'

'I 'earned my stripes' as they say.

Long time ago now.'

'May I ask if it was a hard task, earning them?'

'Ask away. All I'll say is, you can't always be properly rewarded for trying to help someone who needs it. How's that coffee comin', Doc?'

'Soon. Er . . . I did hear that you cared for one of your cellmates when he was poorly. Since then there has been an addendum to that.' He waited but McCall went on washing himself. 'You tried to steal some medicine one of my erring colleagues residing in Yuma suggested might help his condition — twenty lashes was the price, wasn't it?'

McCall paused, glanced over his shoulder. 'Dunno, Doc, passed out when I got to the count of ten.'

'It was foolish, but brave.'

McCall snorted and waded out into deeper water, whistling loudly, then began humming tunelessly.

Sheehan took the hint, sighed, frowning thoughtfully as he dismounted stiffly and led the grey towards the bushes McCall had indicated.

McCall came into the lean-to about fifteen minutes later, hair damp, the old shirt he wore also showing wet patches on his chest and under his arms. His trousers were wet, too. He sniffed. 'Smells OK.'

'It'll be a minute or two yet. This place is difficult to find, even within this short draw.'

'Way I like it. That's dark enough for me, Doc.'

They sipped their brews and McCall unwrapped a cloth that contained the crumbling remains of what had been fresh biscuits at breakfast time. Sheehan shook his head, reaching into his jacket pocket. 'I think I prefer a cheroot — you?'

'Don't smoke. Couldn't rely on a tobacco ration in Yuma so never picked up the habit. When I did get some I traded it for whatever I could.'

Sheehan grunted, staring thoughtfully, and lit a cheroot. 'Something else that makes you different to folk around here.'

McCall looked over the top of his raised cup with a steady gaze. 'I don't see that as any kinda handicap.'

The sawbones exhaled smoke, then shook his head slowly. 'You really don't give a damn, do you?'

'About Keystone folk? Hell! I lived with murderers and rapists and thieves for over three years and preferred their company — your presence excepted, Doc.'

Sheehan smiled thinly. 'You are every bit the hardcase I've heard about. I shouldn't be surprised, of course. You took three years in prison because you helped your friend Ace Morgan, *and* refused to reveal where he had hidden the Wells Fargo money.'

'Friend? He knocked me out, could've killed me, before he took on the posse . . .' His voice trailed off and he smiled wryly. 'Yeah! *You* know he did that so as to make it look like he'd forced his way in and made me help him, don't you? Smart old codger, huh?'

'It was obvious to me. But you had

the guts to come back here — By the way, it was three and a *half* years, wasn't it?'

McCall drained his cup and nodded once. 'You were right about not knowin' how to make a good cup of coffee. Yeah, well, there was a fight in Yuma and I won and the other feller died. Even the guards stood up for me and said he'd forced the issue, so they gave me a token six months extra for 'being disorderly on assembly' or something.'

'Wasn't much of that extra time spent in solitary?'

'Some.' McCall's reply was short. 'You want a second cup? Or you leavin', Doc?'

Sheehan sighed and shook his head. 'I believe I'll pass on the java. But Dana was right: you should have medical attention. I can see at least five wounds that need professional care.'

'No money to spare, Doc. I'm used to taking care of my own needs.'

'I don't doubt it.' The medic had brought in a leather bag and proceeded to open it. 'I'll just help things along a little — *No arguments, dammit!*'

McCall shut his mouth and for the next quarter-hour suffered the doctor's attentions. He admitted — to himself only — that he felt way more comfortable as Sheehan put away his dressings and lotions.

'I won't forget this, Doc.'

'Suit yourself. I've taken the Hippocratic Oath so I am duty-bound to help *anyone* in need of my talents.'

McCall chuckled briefly. 'What happened to Connor, anyway?'

'Oh, he's resting comfortably enough now in my infirmary. That must've been a terrible fight! Extremely brutal.'

'Hell, Doc, in Yuma I'd've been expected to pick up the nearest rock and drop it on his head — talkin' about hardcases . . . '

'Why don't we?' As McCall blinked, Sheehan added, 'I knew your father — briefly — before that bounty hunter shot him in the back. He may've been an outlaw, but he was a decent man.'

'I'm not ashamed of him . . . fact, I'm proud.'

'Easy now, young feller! No need for truculence.'

'Bit of a touchy subject, Doc, sorry.'

Sheehan drained his cup and grimaced. 'Too bad I don't brew better java — or that you don't have anything stronger?'

Ross McCall shook his head, half-smiling. 'Sorry, I need every cent to rebuild this place. When it's finished I'll buy booze, mebbe.'

'Er, why're you so stubborn about staying? Is it because of the Wells Fargo satchel Morgan said he'd hidden here for you? And you haven't located it yet?'

McCall's face was sober now. 'I've searched for that damn satchel till I thought I was turnin' into a gopher, but I dunno where it is. That what really brought you up here?'

Sheehan's old shoulders stiffened and his bearded jaw jutted. He crushed out his cheroot and struggled to his feet.

'I'm beginning to see why you are so disliked around here, young man! There's such a thing as speaking your mind without regard for people's feelings.'

McCall shrugged. 'Just going by instinct, Doc.'

'You don't give an inch, do you?' The medic paused and sighed. 'I suppose you have reasons enough, but it won't get you much sympathy — or help — around here.'

'Don't need either — here or anywhere else.'

'Don't be such a damn fool! You'll need all the help you can get whether you like it or not sometime.'

'Mebbe, but it won't be offered to me on Dark Mesa.'

The medic had his bag now and started to pick his way over the rocks. McCall instinctively started to rise to help the older man, but one glaring look and he sat down again.

He watched Sheehan reach the bottom of the draw and start towards the line of screening brush.

'Doc, thanks for comin'. Sorry I'm such a knot-headed sonofabitch.'

'It may well work against you, young man.' The sawbones paused before parting the brush. 'McCall, how d'you know there's only Wells Fargo money in that satchel? I mean, special delivery letters and important papers are often sent in those secure satchels as well.'

McCall frowned. 'Never even thought about it. Don't matter, anyway, I truly dunno where it is.'

The doctor stared. 'It was just a thought. By the way, d'you know what *Moreno* means in Spanish?'

McCall frowned, face puzzled. 'Just a name . . . like Johnson, or Sheehan.'

'But it does have a definite meaning,' Doc Sheehan added. 'It means 'brown', usually applied to a person's complexion or hair. Sometimes it even substitutes for 'dark'. *Adios.*'

McCall frowned as he watched him leave.

Now what the hell did he tell me that for?

8

Crowding

They almost got him that same night.

It was his own fault and afterwards he couldn't savvy how he had been so slack and plain damn stupid.

Doc Sheehan had left soon after finishing his coffee — and his pow-wow. McCall figured the old medic was either a snoop on his own behalf or acting for someone. He was inclined to give Sheehan the benefit of the doubt but he wasn't sure.

So he went to bed, dog-weary, aching and sunburned despite the covering of charcoal that ought to have given him more protection than it did. His mind was spinning, set in that mode by what Sheehan had told him.

The thing was, he really didn't know anything about the satchel's whereabouts.

Ace Morgan had mentioned Arrrowhead Draw and McCall had paid a visit there, ostensibly moving his small herd in for the grass, but took time to look around. Ace had mentioned traces of an old Spanish religious statue that may have dated back to the Conquistadors' brief foray into this part of the country, so he knew which area Morgan had been in. But he found no trace of any satchel, though there was possible sign of not-too-recent excavation around and under one rock with the crumbling remnants of some kind of old statue on a narrow ledge above.

He wondered about Doc's suggestion there could be something else of value besides money in the satchel. He had no idea what, but it had set his mind racing. Yawning, he dropped a small log into the rock fireplace — the air was getting chilly this late and the lean-to was draughty — and turned in.

He was asleep almost as soon as his head touched the crude pillow he used, made of a roll of worn-out clothes. He would need some more working clothes soon, too, which meant a ride into Keystone and the usual trouble of finding a store that would serve him.

But he was used to it by now and —

There was a sudden crash of gunfire and the angled slab-bark sides of the lean-to shuddered and splintered as the volley caved in the top part of the brush wall. The support beam — a slim sapling, still green and heavy — gave way and fell across his legs, wrenching a brief curse from him. He threw it off and more lead raked the shelter. He snatched his rifle from beside his blankets, kicked out the brush wall he lay against and rolled away as the entire structure caved in with a noisy crash.

Someone laughed in the darkness upslope.

'Nighty-night, you sonofabitch!!' a second voice called hoarsely, slurring the words, and the guns hammered in a long, raking volley.

Ross was rolling and sliding down-slope now and saw that the lean-to was ablaze, having collapsed across his fire. The flames lit the slope where he was and he aided his natural slide by using the butt of the rifle like an oar in a canoe. He grunted with effort as the brass-bound butt dug into loose scree and gravel. The movement set his body rolling instead of sliding, and he found he had a little more control. He snatched at a rock, and the sudden jerk almost wrenched his arm out of its socket as he nearly lost the rifle. He rammed a boot against another rock and felt the sudden jar up his leg like a mule's kick.

He slammed face down, working the rifle lever — and once again heard that drunken laughter from upslope. And more! He heard the crunch of boots as the attackers started down, likely convinced he had smashed his head against a rock and was no longer a problem.

He blinked dust out of his eyes, forced his breathing to steady, and glimpsed their darker shapes against the stars as they stumbled down recklessly.

The rifle butt snugged into his right shoulder and his finger caressed the trigger. The gunshot whiplashed in the night, the long muzzle-flash momentarily blinding him. Not that he needed to see: McCall actually heard the slap of the bullet striking flesh and the yowl of the hit man a moment before the gunman cartwheeled, staggered up drunkenly and began a muttering, ungainly run down the steep slope. By that time, McCall was on the move, crouched low, as he dodged behind a couple of trees that had survived the cabin fire.

He levered another cartridge into the breech, waiting.

The attackers were yelling, panic-edged now, and he rested the rifle against the tree trunk, swung towards the sound and cut loose with three fast shots.

There was a muffled, choking grunt, like a man taking a fist in the throat, followed by a crashing and thrashing, as a body hurtled downslope towards him.

He glimpsed the other raider standing above his sliding comrade and fired hastily, rifle butt jammed against his hip. The man spun violently, his hat flying off, and then went down on all fours, trying to keep from following his partner, who had just about reached McCall's position.

He jumped aside as the wounded gunman tumbled towards him, jabbed out a leg, and staggered as the man struck it. He went down, thrusting, pushing the other into a crevice as he dodged aside, just as the second gunman emptied his rifle wildly in his direction.

He felt the bushwhacker's body jerk under his hand and jumped back, bringing up his own rifle. The man above was running away from him now, his laboured breathing as he fought the steep slope sounding like a distant locomotive.

McCall triggered, but the magazine was empty and he didn't hurry reloading, knowing the dry-gulcher wasn't stopping: all he wanted to do was get away from here.

He turned to the still body at his feet, felt for a heartbeat but found nothing but blood-soaked cloth and torn flesh over the chest area — and with three holes in the back.

Hell! The sheriff isn't going to be too pleased about this, he thought. Nor, probably, would whoever had sent the attackers to crowd him in the first place. *Wonder who that might be . . . ? Ha-ha-ha!*

The dead man was Harp: it was an easy guess who his fleeing companion was.

★ ★ ★

It was a dramatic entrance into Keystone's Main Street early the next morning: McCall on his mount, leading another horse with the dead man loosely roped across the saddle. By the time he reached the law office, Sheriff

116

Fuller was standing on the landing, just licking his cigarette paper, giving it one final twirl before sticking it into a corner of his lined mouth. He had hard eyes in a battered face that showed every one of the nigh-on sixty years Fuller had been wearing it. His clothes were wrinkled, hung on him loosely.

As he shook out the match with one hand, dragged on the cigarette and exhaled without removing it from his mouth his free hand dropped to the butt of the gun he wore somewhat carelessly about his thickening waist.

'You been wakin' up the wildlife again?'

McCall reined down. 'Not me, Sheriff. I was in bed when a couple drunks cut loose with their guns, wrecked my lean-to.'

'That one of 'em?'

'Yeah, Harp Edison. Reckon the other was Link.'

'Heard both were drinkin' free whiskey last night, early, before they quit town.'

'Who was paying for their redeye?'

The sheriff lumbered slowly down the few steps from the landing, walked to the horse holding Harp, grabbed his hair and lifted his head so he could see his face.

'*You* kill him?'

Ross hesitated. 'I don't think so, Sheriff. Thought at first it was me but I only shot at him once, aimed high. But he's got three holes in his back. One slug must've gone right through and bust up his ticker.'

'So you're innocent?'

'I did try to kill him,' McCall admitted with a cold edge to his voice. 'Because that's what he was trying to do to me. But his pard nailed him — my part was self-defence, Sheriff; they attacked me.'

'Uh-huh. But why would his pard shoot him?'

'Think he was shooting at me, but Harp got in the way.'

'Oh? Sure Harp didn't turn to run off and *you* got him in the back?'

'Hey! Dammit, I come in to report a couple of drunks trying to kill me, now you're accusin' me of murder?'

'Just runnin' with the idea. I mean, I've tried to give you a break, son, because you've had it rough, but I gotta take your past into consideration.'

'I don't go round killin' people.' McCall's voice was low and dangerous.

'If we don't count that feller in Yuma, huh?'

'He started the fight! My part was self-defence!'

'Just like you an' Harp, huh?' Fuller held up his hand as he took a deep pull on his cigarette. It caught his throat and he coughed a good deal before he was able to speak again. A small crowd had gathered by now. None of the faces looked particularly friendly to McCall, but that was normal enough for this town. 'You mebbe make a leetle moonshine up there on the mesa, McCall?'

McCall made a disparaging sound and then saw Doc Sheehan in the

119

crowd. 'Doc! You were with me earlier, you know I never had any booze.'

'That right, Doc?'

'Er, none that I saw, Rafe,' the old doctor told the lawman.

'Coulda waited till you left and hit the sauce, couldn't he?'

'I wasn't suggesting that. But I do believe he was considerably upset over the rough deals he's been given — and, I hasten to add, upset rightly so. But whether or not it made him angry enough to shoot someone? No. I would believe self-defence, Sheriff.'

'You din' hear the shootin'?'

The medic frowned. 'I was mighty tired and dozed in the saddle. Could've missed it. Don't recall.'

'Wouldn't've happened to run into Link and Harp and told 'em where to find my lean-to, would you, Doc?'

McCall's voice was harsh and his mouth was tight in the early morning light. Sheehan yawned and gave him a cold look. 'I didn't see anyone to tell anything!'

'Doc, you know my lean-to was up the far end of that dry wash. You had a little trouble findin' it yourself, but the two bozos who shot the place up knew just where to come.'

Sheehan still looked angry. 'It wasn't that hard to find! McCall, I rather enjoyed our meeting earlier — but right now I consider you a pain in the posterior and in case you don't know, that means — '

'Your ass. Yeah, I read Webster's Dictionary mebbe a dozen times in Yuma.'

Sheehan smiled thinly. 'Yes, well, I'll leave you to sort things out with the law; you obviously don't need any help from me.'

McCall watched the crotchety old sawbones stomp away in the direction of his infirmary, almost called him back, but suddenly jumped as he felt a gun barrel pressing against his spine. He jerked as his arms were dragged behind him and the sheriff fumbled with a pair of handcuffs, awkwardly trying to snap them on his wrists.

'Judas Priest, Fuller! You're not gonna lock me up and leave Link on the loose!'

'Quit strugglin', dammit! I got enough trouble handlin' these with my rheumatism. *Goddammit! Stop twistin' and turnin'!* Link won't be on the loose for long. If he's drunk as you say, he'll go someplace to sleep it off and I know all his hidey-holes. You'll have company in the cells before daylight.'

The crowd chuckled and a couple even gave a half-hearted cheer as the sheriff jostled Ross towards the steps, still fighting the stubborn handcuffs. He wrenched Ross's arms up so the younger man grunted in pain. *But damned if he was going to make it easy for the lawman; damned if he was!*

He started to twist and, as the sheriff stumbled, there was a wild Indian yell and a couple of gunshots which scattered the crowd and made Fuller drop to one knee, forgetting the cuffs as he reached for his six-gun.

Wild-eyed, drunk as a skunk, Link

Taggart came thundering down Main on a snorting buckskin mount, shooting into the air, barely able to stay upright in the saddle.

'God*damn!*' yelled Fuller, yanking off his old hat and starting to fling it to the ground but changing his mind and jamming it back on his head. He triggered a shot after the crazy man, yelled at the crowd to get some horses and 'drag Link's sorry ass back here where I can kick it so hard his nose'll bleed for a week!'

'Hey, Sheriff,' someone called, but the lawman swung angrily towards the man.

'Shut up! I want that damn drunk hauled back here and — '

'Sheriff!' the townsman roared. 'Will you open your damned eyes! Goddammit! We were all watchin Ol' Link do his ride so close that' — he paused, then spoke more quietly, but clearly for all to hear — 'we never noticed McCall slip away!' He turned and pointed to where McCall had last been seen: the still-unlocked handcuffs lying now in the grit and dirt on the office steps.

The crowd which had filled the space opened out quickly as Sheriff Fuller stared, his jaw dropping.

This time he threw down his hat and jumped on it.

Several times.

9

Fugitive

Link Taggart put on such a show that hardly an eye in the crowd strayed from him as he galloped down Main, weaving, almost falling from the saddle, leaping his mount on to the boardwalk outside a couple of stores, scattering even more folk going about their early-morning business. A street-front window shattered noisily.

'Sheriff! Sheriff! Stop that maniac!'

That was the cry from running townsfolk, and others on the boardwalk, huddled in doorways. Rafe Fuller hesitated, started forward, hesitated again, dragging his six-gun around and shooting at Link.

Link, crazy with booze, whooped and turned on the lawman.

People ran every which way now and

Link swayed in the saddle as Fuller, trying to savvy what someone was shouting at him about McCall, dropped to one knee, steadied his smoking Colt with both bony, arthritic hands, and fired.

Link was wheeling the terrified horse with foam at its mouth and blood on its flanks from the wildly raking spurs. Sheriff Rafe Fuller's bullet blew the twisting, yelling madman clean out of the saddle.

There was a combined gasp, a short silence as the echoes of the gunshots faded, and then the yelling started again and in the noise, all mention of Ross McCall was lost . . .

★ ★ ★

By that time, he had found himself a horse. He had got rid of the half-connected handcuffs easily enough and before the crowd realized what he was doing he ran down an alley, turned right into another and right again. He found himself at the rear of the saloon with a dozen or so mounts belonging to ranch hands in for a few drinks and a little female company. Several still had rifles in their saddle scabbards. He quickly chose a mount — a lean-flanked roan gelding — and leaped for the stirrup. The animal, being a ranch workhorse, was used to its rider mounting roughly and only grunted as McCall settled in the saddle, wheeled before he had a proper grip on the split reins, and kicked his heels into the flanks.

The horse took off as a cowboy ran out the rear door of the saloon, yelling, groping for his gun. 'Hey! That's my cayuse, you thievin' son-of-a-bee-itch!'

McCall yanked the reins, ran the mount at the startled cowboy. He tried to dodge, but one of the roan's shoulders hit him and knocked him in a heap against the door. But he struggled to one knee as the horse raced on past.

He fired three or four times and the shots attracted the attention of the sweating, confused and flustered sheriff.

'Goh-arrd dammit, Sher'ff!' roared the cowboy, gun empty now. 'That's muh best workhoss! Git a posse after that damn thief! An' I mean right now!'

The crowd yelled agreement and, as Fuller blinked, trying to make out all the instructions and suggestions being flung at him, another voice said, calmly, 'McCall's cleared the town boundary, Sheriff. I recommend that you activate an official Fugitive Warrant and get a posse after him — immediately.'

Fuller, still flustered, looked at Virgil Caldwell, his lips parted. Then he suddenly nodded and called for a posse. 'Draw up that warrant, Virgil!'

'County payin' for posse time, Rafe?' asked someone astutely.

Fuller scowled. 'Yeah, yeah! Let's get after that — damn killer.' He glanced across the street and saw that Harp Edison's body lay half on the boardwalk and half in the gutter. It angered him as he cast around for Link. The man must still be alive for he had crawled into a doorway and sprawled there now, holding a blood-streaked hand against his chest, sobered up — very much so. 'Someone get Link to Doc's an' make Harp decent! Then let's go!' roared Fuller.

'Dead or alive?' a man called, making the others pause in their rush for mounts.

Fuller looked sharply at Caldwell, who solemnly shook his head. 'Not advisable at this stage, Sheriff.'

'Which makes the sonofa mighty lucky!' gritted Fuller and, breathing hard, he started across the street towards his office and the small stables behind it.

By then, there was only a thin haze of dust hanging in the early-morning air to mark the fugitive's passage.

★　★　★

Well, that's done it! The thought kind of slammed through McCall's mind as he crouched over the workhorse's straining neck: it sure did respond quickly to the demands of reins and spurs, sometimes even seemed to anticipate its rider's desires.

The rifle was in the scabbard but he had lost his Colt somewhere. He could hear water splashing in the canteen slung behind his left leg on the saddle, but a quick feel of the barely bulging saddle-bags didn't give him confidence in how much food they might be carrying. Likely only a little jerky for emergencies. Even though these cowboys worked the Candlelight Ranges 'most every day of their lives, they would play it safe: these hills were a pure bitch to get lost in once off the known trails, and if a man was hurt, couldn't move much, a little grub to nibble on and a drink of canteen water would surely boost his spirit.

Luckily for Ross McCall, he *knew* much of the country: since coming here he had made a point of studying it. His father had told him once: 'Kid, you go into wild country, you make sure you know a way out before you get in there

too deep. Fact, *find* a way out before-
hand if you can. Yeah, I know, it can be
a lotta trouble and sometimes you got
law or someone breathin' down your
neck, but it's worth the time: take my
word for it.'

Hc had always remembered that and
had taken the advice.

By now, after all this time in the
ranges, he had several escape routes
figured out. 'Yuma precautions', it was
called . . . or *anti*-Yuma.

From a ridge he saw the ragged posse
Fuller had cobbled together, way back,
just riding towards the ranges because
they knew that's where he would make
for. *And* they knew he could easily
outrun or outwit them in there, too.

But if the county was paying the posse
by the day, well, that part was OK. Even
the few measly cents the county paid
would soon mount up as the days slid
by.

McCall smiled tightly, said, half-aloud,
'Come on, gents! Lemme show you just
what scenic beauty and mighty rugged

country you have on your doorstep — and know as much about as you can flick into a gnat's eye!'

Most of the men were from town, more eager for the sheriff's meagre posse pay than studying the country they would have to hunt over. They didn't know the hills away from the worn trails but figured they would have McCall locked up in one of Fuller's cells by sundown . . . or, with luck, might even stretch the time until tomorrow's sundown.

Instead, they were about to have a lesson in survival . . . a hard lesson.

★　★　★

He let them see him riding along the ridge into brush and, when they swung towards the slopes that would bring them up there, he chuckled, shaking his head slowly.

Likely Sheriff Rafe Fuller would take it easier — he was a mite old now for rough riding in such country and would soon drop back — but doggedly keep trying to out-think McCall.

It was the eager beavers he wanted to spot him and ride after him recklessly.

Within an hour, the posse was hopelessly lost.

They milled about in the dead-end canyon he had led them to. A couple of the bewildered townsmen, a little more cagey than their companions, waited within view of the entrance, not liking the high-walled canyon much.

It probably seemed safe enough, with so many of them, but McCall knew there were a lot of insecure boulders on the steep slopes just outside the rugged, narrow entrance. He was far above, had already used a deadfall sapling to prise loose a boulder taller than himself and leave it precariously balanced above a nest of smaller rocks below.

Once he figured all the posse was in the canyon — there was thick brush between him and the trail he had left below and he couldn't be sure — he jumped for the high-angled deadfall jammed beneath the big boulder. He kicked in mid-air as he struggled to bring it down with his weight. When, within a couple of minutes, he hadn't succeeded, he took the lariat from the saddlehorn of the workhorse, tossed and tightened a loop over the highest end of the deadfall and backed up the straining but obedient animal.

'Nothing like a willing workhorse,' he told himself as the sapling creaked and cracked, giving him a moment or two of gut-knotting panic as he thought it might snap.

It didn't. It moved as he wanted it to and the boulder rocked past the point of precarious balance, groaned as it rolled to the rim of the ledge and dropped, smackdown solidly into the piled rocks beneath.

He felt the slope tremble and even reached out to steady himself against a tree trunk as, momentarily, it felt as if the whole mountain was sliding away. But that was only a brief illusion and next came a tremendous crash followed by a growling, roaring sound as the boulders jarred loose and thundered over the edge like a massive stone waterfall, blocking the canyon entrance.

He couldn't see the pandemonium caused because of the choking, blinding dust, but he vaguely heard the shouts of alarm and anger. Someone in his panic even began shooting — at what, he couldn't even guess. With a small smile he turned back to the panting work-mount . . . then stopped dead in his tracks.

Sheriff Rafe Fuller, looking more than a mite distressed with sweat streaming from him and chest heaving like a black-smith's bellows from his climb up the slope, stood there with a cocked pistol.

McCall hesitated, but reluctantly raised his hands, asking, 'Where the hell did you come from?'

'I been livin' here for a lot more time than you spent in Yuma, boy. Soon's I seen your trail was leadin' to Sawbuck Canyon, I knew what you was about. Used the same ploy myself once — aw, must've been five years ago now — can't

135

recall 'zactly. Trapped the whole damn Jacksonville Bunch under Buzz Finlay. Them we didn't shoot, we strung up before sundown the same day.'

McCall was impressed. 'I heard about that, but not your name. But this time, it's your posse blocked in, Sheriff.'

'Ah, won't hurt 'em none to spend a cold, hungry night tryin' to get loose. I'll send someone from the Mines Office up here with some dynamite tomorrow.'

'Meantime . . . ?' asked McCall carefully as the pistol menaced him.

'Meantime, drop that rifle an' I'll take you back to town. That cell I had ready for you is still there waitin' . . . Now, you ain't gonna make trouble for me, are you, boy . . . ?'

McCall sighed heavily, dropped the rifle. 'Not me.'

Fuller nodded, and waved the six-gun for him to move carefully. Then he saw the fugitive suddenly stiffen, looking past the lawman's shoulder.

'What're you — ?'

'He mightn't give you no trouble,

Fuller, but I will!'

As Rafe Fuller spun quickly, almost overbalancing, there was a gunshot and the lawman was flung back into the rocks, sprawled, rolled off into a small crevice and didn't move. Blood smeared the rock he rested against, trickled from one corner of his slack mouth.

Lee Connor grinned at McCall through the gun-smoke. The fugitive had frozen his own movements, shocked by the lawman's murder.

'Now, what you want to go and do that for, McCall, ol' hoss? Shootin' poor Fuller down in cold blood that way!'

McCall raised his gaze from the sheriff's body.

'That how you're gonna tell it?'

'Hey, I just witnessed it, din' I? Someone asks me, I gotta tell what I saw, don't I?'

'Think anyone'll believe you?'

'Hell, yeah! You're a fugitive, an' you just dropped a rock wall into that canyon, trapping Fuller's posse. He caught you redhanded, but you was quicker with your gun and . . . ' He shrugged and nodded briefly to the still lawman. 'Yeah, I reckon folk'll find that easy enough to believe — considering your background.'

He was right, dammit! Folk *would* find it mighty easy to believe.

'I know what that'll get *me*, Connor, but what'll it get you?'

Connor, face still showing the battering he had taken in their fight, the left side covered with a lint gauze square that oozed a little ointment, smiled. His mouth took on a crooked shape because of the stiffness of his facial wounds and a swollen jaw.

'It'll get me right back in Señor Moreno's good books — which I need to do seein' as this chore is takin' longer than we figured.'

'How'll that work? You somehow get me back to Keystone and they're likely to string me up — and I get the notion that ain't exactly what Moreno had in mind.'

''Course not, he wants to talk to you,

then he'll tell you what he wants.'

'Which is?'

'He don't tell me all his business. But it works this way, McCall: I take you to him and you do what he wants, and you get clear of this country. You make a fuss an' I guarantee I'll convince the Keystone folk you killed ol' Fuller and, like you said, they'll string you up — pronto. You want time to think it over?'

McCall stared back coldly and, after a long minute, shook his head once. Connor smiled again, just as crookedly, but there was a definite gleam of triumph in his usually bleak eyes. He chuckled.

'Kinda glad I never listened to that ol' sawbones — said I was still too poorly to be leavin' his infirmary.' He sobered suddenly and spat, eyes narrowing. 'I told him I had this urge to get after you for puttin' me in there, and he better not try to stop me or he'd be needin' one of his own beds . . . so, here we are.' He cupped one hand behind his left ear. 'Posse's hollerin' and panickin'. Pretty smart move that, blockin' off the canyon. But what about you an' me? I gonna shoot you an' throw you to the posse, or you gonna come along an' meet Mr Moreno?'

McCall, lips a thin, tight line in his hard face, said simply,

'Guess.'

10

Troubled Trail

There was still chaos down in the canyon with the posse trapped. Two of the men, Simm Barcross, the Keystone blacksmith, and Carl Devlin, the stageline agent, had explored all around the perimeter of the canyon and agreed there was no possible way out on horseback — unless you had a case of dynamite to blast a passage. The walls were steep and smooth, mighty hard to climb.

'The sonofa's bottled us up good an' proper,' announced Devlin. 'We're here until someone comes lookin' for us.'

'Why would they do that?' asked a smallish man with an eyepatch. 'We're a posse, ain't we? They dunno if we're gonna be out ten hours or ten days!'

'Ten *days*'ll do me!' shouted a man

from the cooper's works. 'Long as they keep payin' us!'

There was laughter and cusses, the latter urging them to do something positive! 'Keep your jokes till later!'

'Well, where the hell's Rafe Fuller? If he hadn't been drag-assin' an' kept up with us we mightn't be stuck here. An' what was that gunshot we heard?'

Big Simm Barcross held up his muscled arms. 'Doughball's right, gents, Rafe should be out there by now. He can't do nothin' alone but — I'll volunteer to try to climb up that avalanche the kid dropped into the pass. Reckon I can do it an' find out what's goin' on.'

'Yeah, you could do it, Simm, but what the hell good will it do? You'll be afoot if Rafe ain't there an' it's one helluva walk back to town.'

'We heard that gunshot,' pointed out a man with a close-cropped red beard. 'Rafe musta been signallin' us.'

'Coulda been the damn kid!'

'Well, what would he be shootin' at?'

'The hell's it matter? Long as Simm

can get his hoss away from him.'

'Reckon I can do that if he's still hangin' around.' And, as they all started talking at once again, the blacksmith waved his arms until they stopped. 'I don't aim to walk back to town nohow! Hell, we're in cattle country, gents! Ranches out here are a lot closer'n town.'

'Still mighty rugged to have to slog through these hills on foot to get to any of 'em, Simm!'

'Yeah, yeah, but I figure I get me up on to the rim I'll start a brushfire. The smoke's bound to bring in some ranny makin' sure his cows ain't in any danger. Or even Rafe: he's gotta be close to here by now.'

They discussed the idea and the overwhelming result was that what Simm Barcross said made sense.

'Hey, Simm,' called a young ranny who did roustabout work among the saloons in town, 'see if you can hook up with the Double Five. That Dana Cooke not only lives up to her name, and serves mighty good grub, but she's good-lookin' to boot!'

More laughter sent Simm on his way and he spat on his big, calloused hands, rubbed them briskly together, and started to look for a safe way up the jumbled boulders that towered before him.

One wrong move and he could bring down twenty tons of rock on top of him. He crossed himself before starting.

* * *

Lee Connor had the upper hand.

McCall could see there was no use fighting this cold-blooded ranny who had just so casually killed Sheriff Rafe Fuller — a basically good man, the sheriff, a mite slow on the uptake and getting on in years, but one with good intentions. He didn't deserve to die at the hands of a skunk like Connor.

But maybe that could be set right — sometime. *Soon!*

'Get on your hoss mighty easy,'

Connor ordered, watching with narrowed eyes, thumb holding back the hammer on his Colt. 'Now, hold them rein ends between your teeth and keep your hands shoulder high; you're forkin' a cow pony so you can guide him with your knees.'

McCall obeyed, wanting to make some sort of reply, if not objection, but with the foul leather rein ends clamped between his teeth it wasn't easy to do more than make a few grunting sounds. He badly wanted to spit, and knew his arms would feel like leaden weights before they had covered a mile. *A ride to remember — if he survived . . .*

Connor swung easily aboard his long-legged black and settled into leather, his cocked six-gun never wavering.

'Comfy?' he asked with a short, hard laugh. 'Got us a tolerably long ride ahead of us, McCall; you wanna get to meet Moreno, you'll do just like I say, or I'm gonna have to explain how come I killed you. The killin' part'll be sweet enough, but not explainin' to him, so ride easy, 'cause if I have to stop you from makin' a run for it, I swear I'll shoot you through both feet then make you walk to Keystone.'

'You've got such comfortin' ideas.'

Connor's eyes pinched down a little more and he jerked the Colt's barrel towards a sloping path running off to the left. 'That way.'

McCall kneed the obedient roan towards the path and saw out of the corner of his eye that Connor was moving to get behind him.

At the same time, he saw a movement at the edge of the landslide he had sent crashing down into the canyon to trap the posse.

A man, a big man, who, apparently when he spotted McCall and Connor, went to ground mighty fast, dropping out of sight between two rocks, his grey hat showing last of all.

It brought Connor up half-standing in the stirrups now, gun ready to throw down on a target. 'What was that?'

'What's wrong, bad boy?' McCall asked, half choking with the reins. 'Never seen a rock squirrel before?'

Connor gave him a cold look. 'It was too damn quick to tell what the hell it was!'

'It was a squirrel, all right, there's nut-bearing bushes all over these slopes.'

Connor frowned, then grunted and waved his gun.

'Never mind the wildlife! Just ride on up that slope! An' get them reins back in your mouth properly!'

McCall obeyed: he hoped whoever that had been — and it must have been someone from the posse trying to find a way out — had seen them both. *If* he ever came to trial over Fuller's death, he reasoned, at least there was now a witness that Connor was with him, holding him under a gun, and it was no longer a foregone conclusion that he, Ross McCall, had been the one to murder the old sheriff.

But, of course, he had to live through

this thing, wherever Connor was taking him, for it to matter at all.

'Hit that narrow ledge trail!' Connor suddenly snapped, making him start a little. 'I'm droppin' back a few yards, so don't get any notions of waitin' round a bend to push me over the edge.'

'Now *there's* an idea!' McCall mumbled around the reins.

Connor scowled. 'You try it, you're dead!'

'And if I don't try?' His words were almost unintelligible because of the now sodden leather. He felt queasy.

Connor chuckled. 'I guess you're dead anyway! But that'll be up to Moreno.'

'I can hardly wait to meet him.'

'Ah, an' he's waitin' to meet you! He's a patient man, Señor Moreno, but you got him all antsy, squirmin' in his chair, and he don't like that.' Connor's face brightened abruptly as he added, 'I don't think you're gonna find much of a welcome where we're goin', mister! Not much — at — all!'

As McCall scowled, Connor gestured with the gun.

'Get them reins back in your mouth! Last time I'm gonna tell you!'

'They make me want to puke.'

'Hell, I figured they'd be reeeaaal tasty.'

'For a hog, mebbe! All that horse sweat in the leather and hell knows what else kinda mess they been in.'

'Aw, well, weren't that thoughtless of me!' Connor's face hardened. The gun barrel jumped an inch. 'Get 'em back in your mouth an' *keep* 'em there!'

McCall sighed. 'I have to spit every so often.'

'Swallow it!' Connor's grin was tight and unrelenting. 'Get — 'em — *in*!'

'Goddammit, Connor, I — ' McCall mumbled unclearly around the soggy rein ends, dark juices trickling over his chin now, his stomach rebelling.

'You'll do just like I say! Or I'll shoot an ear off — how you like that, huh? You've marked me for life, you sonofabitch!' He touched the lint on his scarred face. 'Time I did somethin' for you! Start chawin'!'

He raised the pistol, sighting, and notched the hammer back to full cock, the barrel inches from McCall's face. It was so close he could see specks of holster dust on the tips of the bullets in the cylinder. 'Git yourself a mouthful an' *swallow*!'

McCall grimaced, chomped, feeling — and tasting — the well-used leather, his mouth filling. He bulged his cheeks and made another grimace. Connor liked that, laughed out loud, throwing back his head slightly —

Then McCall squirted the mouthful of foul slop squarely into Connor's face, aiming for his eyes, but missing — just. The killer wasn't prepared for it and some of the liquid splashed into his eyes anyway. He swept up a hand swiftly, jerking his head as his vision blurred, eyes stinging now,

McCall leaned forward quickly and brought his aching arms around, snatching at the pistol. He fumbled and

150

Connor fought back, coming out of his shock. McCall lifted an arm and drove an elbow against the man's still-healing broken nose. Connor howled and spilled sideways. McCall used his heels, ramming them into the roan's flanks, which were tough but unmarked, as he wasn't wearing spurs. Maybe the animal appreciated that for it surged forward like a four-legged bullet, ramming into Connor's startled mount and setting it stumbling back at least a yard.

The trail was narrow and a steep slope dropped away from the edge. Connor's horse stepped off into nothing but air . . .

There was a wild yell and a whinny, the anguished cries, human and animal, mingling, to be drowned out by Connor's Colt firing, just the once, before it jumped from his grip. It hit the slope and skidded away. Moments later, both Connor and his horse toppled off the narrow trail.

They hit hard, a cloud of dust rising, but he stayed in the saddle, trying to ride the horse on to its feet enough so it could get a grip. McCall didn't stop to see the result. He leapt his roan at them, and Connor yelled as flailing hoofs took him in the back and sent him spinning out of the saddle. The jar knocked his mount on to its side and it went down, already sliding, skidding, whinnying in panic with wildly flailing legs.

McCall urged the roan along the narrow trail, unarmed, wanting only to get out of here now. The cow pony was sure-footed and leaned into a bend just as a bloody-faced Connor lurched up awkwardly to his knees, bringing his rifle to his shoulder. McCall saw it all out of the corner of his eye as the roan reached the sharpest part of the bend which took him away from the rising slope background and silhouetted him against the hot blue sky.

Just as Connor fired.

He felt the horse shudder under him and its head jerked as a second bullet thudded home. He threw himself from the saddle, hit the slope and scrabbled madly to get out of the way of the thrashing animal coming down on top of him. He launched himself bodily, so close a hoof cracked him on the side of the head, dazing him, and then the roan was past, still on its back, trailing blood.

McCall was hardly aware that he was still sliding down the steep slope. More bullets spat dust around his tumbling body as Connor worked the rifle lever frantically.

All he could think of was: that was a magnificent horse, that roan. It shouldn't've had to die like that at the hands of a cold-blooded mongrel like Lee Connor . . .

That was two he owed him for! Rafe and the roan.

Then he hit a flat ledge and his body jarred painfully before he hurtled into space.

And just then, Lee Connor ran out of ammunition.

He glared through the blood running into his eyes, wiped it away with a savage, scrubbing gesture, spat in the direction McCall had gone as he fumbled cartridges from his belt loops.

'I hope you ain't got more'n an inch of whole hide left on your lousy bones, you bastard!' He looked towards his dazed and snorting mount as it lurched to its feet, coat covered in blood-streaked dust. Grunting, Connor used the rifle to help him up, lurched towards the hurt animal.

'Let's go check him out, you damn crowbait!'

The horse was skittish and earned several cuffs across the ears and a punch in the throat before the angry Connor swung into saddle.

'Think I'll kill that sonofabitch anyway, worry later about explainin' to Moreno! Now *move*!'

11

Downriver

McCall had had the wind knocked out of him by the drop off the ledge. He spun and slid down further, but there was loose soil this time and he was able to dig in his heels, slow down enough to throw himself behind a line of boulders.

He heard a yell upslope, didn't bother glancing in that direction: there was only one person it could be. He concentrated on staying low and flattened instinctively as two bullets chipped the rocks sheltering him.

Prone again, he started rolling and, as soon as he figured he was out of range, rammed in his heels and elbows, twisted painfully and hurled himelf on to a slope steeper than he had encountered so far.

The world was a blur, he dropped so fast. He didn't even hear the rifle, if, indeed, Connor was using it, but he guided himself around the line of rocks, hoping he was in the area he wanted to be and — *yes!* The slope continued down, but also angled away to the left. With a grunt that hurt his throat he propelled himself on to this side slope, yelled involuntarily as he saw he was dropping through space again but this time with the creek rushing past below.

He didn't know the depth of water and gave up a quick prayer that it was deep. A very strong current ran here, for the creek had come tumbling and roaring down from the high ridge and had actually cut a channel in this side of the slope. He kicked wildly — and futilely — in mid-air as he realized he was going to hit the mountain first — and his hurtling body would be flung like a stone from a catapult, probably broken like an overcooked biscuit.

He would more than likely land in the creek, *but* there were deadfalls and washaways with jagged tree branches and rocks reaching up through the muddy water down there. *Talk about between a rock and a hard place!*

Breath was smashed from his lungs, despite his vain attempt at trying to change direction in mid-air. He hit the very edge of the high bank, feet first, his knees almost ramming back up into his face.

He had struck on an overhang and his weight violently dislodged about a hundred pounds of falling dirt and stones to accompany him as he plunged towards the creek.

Already dazed, the shock of the water did little to bring him out of it. But instinct took over and he struck out in an awkward swimming motion, half-blinded with grit, not even sure which direction he was heading. He ducked his head under, deliberately opening his eyes and feeling them sting as the moving water not only washed the grit away but rasped at his eyeballs.

He sucked in a deep gulp of air and frog-dived. He thought he heard the slap of a bullet only inches above his head, but, by then, he was plunging for the creek bottom. Before his wildly scrabbling hands felt the first sub-merged twigs and general muck, he was surrounded by shots popping randomly into the water about his upper body. When he figured Connor had emptied the weapon he half-rolled, kicked his legs, and thrust away horizontally.

By now his lungs were bursting and everything was taking on a red tinge that alternated with what appeared to be black smoke. He had to surface no matter what the risk.

He burst through, gagging and spitting, dizzy from the lack of oxygen, glimpsed Connor standing beside his horse on a higher part of the bank, fumbling to reload.

Then he realized he had surfaced between two battered, semi-submerged tree trunks. He wasted no time in grab-bing a slippery branch on one, kicked against the other and set it adrift. He pressed his face against the surface of the water. The current had the tree in its grip now, whirled it through a tangled bush with a snake clinging to the upper branches, and carried it past Connor's position.

McCall submerged, ducking directly under the log, tightening his grip, and held his breath until he thought his lungs would burst. His head emerged in the midst of a tangle of broken branches; luckily the snake had gone now.

Gasping, he stared up through the leaves, saw Connor, rifle apparently reloaded, in the same spot, but facing away from him. He wanted to laugh, smothered the urge.

He'd made it! Connor had missed seeing him go past behind the tree trunk and was still looking for him upstream.

Even as McCall had the thought, he saw the killer savagely spur-rake his mount and ride back the other way, half-standing in the stirrups as his hard eyes raked the creek for any sign of his quarry.

Then McCall and his tree trunk were whipped around a surging bend and rushed downstream. It was still a long way before the creek reached the valley below and he reckoned his aching body would be one huge bruise — *if* he got that far!

As he clung desperately to the log, now gathering speed, he wondered if he would survive the series of rugged drops and falls — and the rapids! — between him and the valley floor.

The only way to find out was to hang on and hope.

★　★　★

Connor knew he had messed up. But admitting his mistake did nothing for his mood. His blood was up and the only thing to calm him down would be to spill someone else's.

Damn McCall! He couldn't just disappear into thin air! But kill-crazy though he was, he still had enough sense to think it through logically.

Nursing the rifle, he climbed up on a rock and sat there with the weapon across his knees, studying the raging water and the flotsam dotting its surface.

That was the answer, of course! Those goddamn floating logs and bushes, even a couple of dead cows polluting the river, swirling from this side to that, spinning in a whirlpool, ramming a rock where the water stormed into spray.

'Christ! You could hide an army patrol out there!' he breathed, gasping a little. His nose was swollen from where McCall had hit him and he tasted stale blood in the back of his throat. He spat to windward, stood on top of the rock, looking for a big tree he recalled swirling around as it passed him with a few bushes caught up in its branches.

'Perfect hiding place for the sonofa!' he gritted aloud, then kicked at a rock and hurt the side of his foot. He was in such a rage he almost shot the rock, but enough sanity prevailed and instead he started limping along the creek bank.

With a little effort he managed to

out-pace the current and draw slightly ahead of drifting, crashing debris, but it revealed no sign of his quarry. Then Connor heard — before he saw — the thundering roar as the creek plunged down to the next level. He stopped, breath hissing through clenched teeth as he smiled fixedly.

'Well, McCall, ol' hoss,' he panted. 'You are entirely welcome to take that there plunge! Don't think I'll even bother lookin' for your body. From that height, I doubt your dear ol' ma would recognize what's left of you when you hit them rocks!' He flicked a mocking salute from the crumpled brim of his hat. '*Adios*, farewell, goodbye, so long — an' all the rest of it! You are . . . gone, you bastard! An' good riddance!'

He even managed a scratchy kind of whistle as he turned back from the edge after cautiously leaning out a little to see more clearly what waited below.

His smile broadened: just as he thought. A cauldron foamed and raged and swirled at the bottom of the first drop, and there were three more to follow, though less steep, before the creek reached the valley level.

By the time Mr Ross McCall was tossed out of that white thunder he would be nothing but bloody pulp.

Just what he needed, too — report to Moreno that regrettably, Ross McCall was killed in an accident, drowned while trying to escape . . . unavoidable, Señor!

Yeah! He might get a cussing-out but nothing more.

He even patted his horse's neck before setting it at a casual pace paralleling the watercourse.

* * *

'I think he's dead,' panted the cowboy in the sodden chaps and trousers, wiping a wet shirtsleeve across his eyes. He spoke in ragged gasps after his clumsy swim in the fast-moving water to retrieve the body they had seen being jostled and flung about in the current.

'I dunno, Hank, thought I heard him

kinda gurgle,' said his companion, another cowboy but drier, and not wearing chaps.

'Just the water in him sloppin' around.' Squatting, water oozing from the leather chaps as his legs bent, Hank turned the unconscious man's head to one side. 'Look at it run outa his mouth, Stew! Like a pump faucet.'

'Bet he's glad to get rid of that — Hello! He's comin' round, by Godfrey!'

The rescued man coughed and vomited up murky creek water with such suddenness that Hank fell backwards and sat on the wet sand.

Stew, shorter, but wider in the shoulders, knelt swiftly and lifted the limp body, grunting as he draped the half-drowned McCall over a log, face down.

'The hell you doin' . . . ?'

'Seen my old man do this with a prize heifer got caught in a flood once. Squeezed its ribs and squirted out the river water. Later, it made him hundreds of bucks in prizes.'

Following the instructions of the wide-shouldered man, Hank held McCall's arms out straight, working them up and down, forward and backward, while Stew placed his spread hands at the bottom of the rib cage and squeezed until McCall coughed and vomited again and again, groaning now.

It took all of twenty minutes before he raised his head, eyes dazed, dribbling creek water as he looked around.

'Grrrr . . . ?'

'Same to you, feller!' said the heard-breathing Stew, massaging his hands. 'Hey, Hank, I think we done it, he's gonna live.'

'Still looks three-parts dead to me.'

'Well, what you expect? He got washed over that rim and into *that!*' He pointed to the boiling water at the base of the rocky drop.

'Damn lucky you ask me.' Hank leaned forward. 'You feelin' lucky, feller?'

McCall stared blankly, then his mouth twitched and he nodded. 'Real . . . lucky,' he rasped, starting to cough again.

'It's that feller from Dark Mesa! There was a posse after him, I heard.

What we gonna do with him, Stew?'

'Take him to Dana, I reckon. She'll know the best thing to do. Hey, you feel like a ride, mister?'

McCall looked at him soberly, took his time answering. 'I feel like curling up and sleepin' for a week.'

The cowboys grinned. He put out a hand and grabbed Hank's arm as he made to move away. 'Thanks for draggin' me out, boys. Er — wouldn't have a drink of canteen water, would you? Got a lousy taste in my mouth . . . need to rinse it out . . . '

Both cowboys broke into laughter.

* * *

But Lee Connor wasn't feeling so happy.

His first thoughts about reporting to Moreno that McCall had been unavoidably drowned were fading fast.

It would be true, but that wouldn't matter to Moreno. If he didn't want to believe it, then it wouldn't make any difference what he was told. He wasn't a man who confided in his underlings and Connor was little more than a hired gun. A *good* hired gun and one who enjoyed many more privileges than other hardcases on the man's payroll, but he was still expected to do *all* his chores successfully.

And the fact of the matter was that Moreno didn't want McCall dead — leastways, not yet. There was something he required of the man first. After that — well, anyone could use him for target practice.

But not until he had carried out the chore Moreno desired first.

Connor felt himself break out in a cold sweat as he played the scene — in his mind — where he told Moreno about McCall drowning over and over.

'*No, sir!*' he said aloud with a gulp. 'Uh-uh!'

He wanted McCall dead, but Moreno had a use for him so Señor Moreno had priority.

Connor sweated and ducked low-swinging branches, even rode down and crossed a narrow section of the creek at one stage and, finally, after almost an hour's ride, he found a way down and came out near the raging cauldron that he figured would've — *should've* — drowned the sonofabitch!

He looked past the thundering water, easing in slightly, felt its stinging lash and quickly withdrew. He got down on hands and knees, crawled on his belly, but couldn't get a really clear view of the hidden area.

He got to his feet, dusting off wet sand and cursing as some fell down his shirt collar and scratched his neck. Then he paused, knelt again and looked beneath a column of water that splashed off some rocks. Just beyond it, caught up on one of the half-submerged rocks was something that caught his eye — dark, sodden, more or less shapeless.

About half of the old blue shirt McCall had been wearing!

'By God! The sonofa must've hit somewhere along here!' He looked around, head filling with the thunder of the falling column of water: this was almost, *almost*, like a kind of room, off to one side — a deep patch of sand and . . . something else. Huge!

'Hell almighty! It's that damn log with the bushes caught up in it! Judas Priest, the bastard could still be alive after all!'

His stomach was jumping with a rush of nervous tension, when, crawling now to get past a rock, he saw all the sand churned up, a broken spur, a torn strip of leather from workaday chaps with a battered concha still attached.

Well, *that* sure didn't belong to McCall . . .

Breathing faster now, hand tightening instinctively on his rifle, he cast about him, found rough tracks that led past some brush into a clearing where he saw fresh horse dung; he smelled it first, then came to a mound of it.

More sign told him there were two horses, one going off with a load, like —

'Double load! One man ridin', the other hanging on behind — or draped over the saddle.' He spat savagely. 'Them damn cowpokes I seen working over t' other side of the creek! Jesus! But that McCall has the luck of the Irish! The sonofa's been rescued!'

12

The Best Thing?

Virgil Caldwell glanced up sharply from the writing pad he was using as his office door opened and his middle-aged, spinsterish secretary stood there.

He frowned and looked about to swear, but, instead, said harshly, 'I thought I told you I wasn't to be dis — '

He didn't complete the last word as the stubbled face of a dishevelled Lee Connor appeared behind the woman who was licking her lips preparing to speak. But she didn't get a chance to say anything.

Caldwell, snappy and annoyed, letting it show, said 'Very well, Miss Garner, that'll be all. You'd better come in.'

This last was to Connor and it made the man who had done some really hard riding to get here angry — Caldwell hardly ever addressed him by name, Christian or sur!

Connor trudged in, managing to kick some creek mud and sand on to the carpet, bringing a flush to Caldwell's face.

'Careful, dammit! This carpet is imported from — '

He swallowed the rest as Connor deliberately turned his filthy boots side-on, taking his time scraping off much of the accumulated muck. He looked at Caldwell with a crooked smile as he dropped into a visitor's chair with a thump.

'Nice to see you, too, Counsellor.' He leaned forward, lifted the lid of the big silver cylinder holder in front of the outraged Caldwell and helped himself to a fat cigar. 'Got a light?'

Caldwell's eyes narrowed but he swallowed the retort he had been about to make. Connor was carrying his rifle and he held it in his free hand so that it — casually or by design — slanted slightly, the muzzle pointing at Caldwell's head.

His hand shook as he struck a vesta taken from another silver holder near the big cylinder and held it for Connor to light up.

'You had better have a *very* good reason for this kind of behaviour in my office, Connor.'

'That's *Mister* Connor, but never you mind, I'll let it ride.'

'Why are you here? Mr Moreno's orders were very clear that you were to concentrate on McCall.'

'Moreno's a long way from here and he won't know I came in for a break — unless someone blabs — will he?'

Caldwell flinched involuntarily at the look on Connor's face. He cleared his throat. 'Well, now you're here, state your business.'

Connor sucked on the cigar, exhaled the smoke, staring into the aromatic cloud as if for inspiration. When the attorney looked ready to explode, Connor said, with maddening timing, just as the other's mouth opened to speak, 'That damn McCall . . . ' He let the words hang.

Caldwell forced himself to stay calm, eased back in his chair. 'What about him?'

'Near drowned in the creek which is runnin' a bumper after that rain upstream, but couple of Double Five cowpokes dragged him out and pumped the water outa him. He was alive when they rode out with him, headin' for that Cooke ranch.'

'Did you see all this?'

'Some. Read most from the sign they left.'

'Then you don't know for sure he's still alive! They may've been taking him somewhere else to . . . kill him.'

'Why the hell would they go to the trouble of pullin' him outa the damn creek if they wanted him dead?'

'Perhaps they'd hoped to interrogate him first.'

'Hogwash. Anyway, I followed, way back, holed up on that big butte that looks down across Double Five's holding corrals. The woman was there and it was obvious she was interested. They all went up to the house, the two rannies almost carryin' McCall, his toes draggin' in the dust.'

'So he's hurt?'

Connor snorted. 'Ought to be dead! Getting washed all that way down the creek and over the falls . . . Yeah, he's alive. But it don't mean he has to stay that way. Fact, him goin' to the Cooke place could be the best thing; I can pick him off anytime he pokes his nose out the door.'

Caldwell looked at him severely. 'And you think that Mr Moreno would approve of such action?'

'McCall's a big pain in Moreno's butt, ain't he? If he don't want him shot, I can soon rig things when he's out on the range and make it look like an accident.'

Caldwell arched his eyebrows, surprisingly impressed with this notion. But then his face sobered and he shook his head. 'McCall is of more value to Moreno alive than dead. I'm not saying he wouldn't like to see him dead, only that he needs McCall to perform a special job for him first.'

'Well, hell, I guess I can wait, but it sure does seem a damn pity to pass up the chance to — '

'It's a blessing in disguise, actually,' Caldwell cut in abruptly, enjoying the puzzlement on Connor's face. 'Both of us would . . . benefit . . . if we helped Señor Moreno achieve what he wants, you know.'

'An' how the hell do we do that? When we dunno what it is?'

'We use something called pressure, Connor. Bring enough of the right kind to bear and almost any man will bend under it and do what's wanted of him.'

Connor frowned. 'You're losin' me.'

'Ah, but *I* know where we're going, so you just sit there and listen for a few minutes and it won't be long before you have McCall in your sights — with Moreno's full blessing.'

Connor still looked puzzled, but shrugged, eased back in the chair, hooking one heel over his other leg.

'Better tell me what you got in mind.'

'Yes, I believe I better had. Shall we discuss it over a drink?'

'Judas! You *must* want my help bad! Make mine a double, Counsellor — a big double. OK?'

*   *   *

'You're very lucky that arm isn't broken, Mr McCall.'

He looked up at Dana Cooke as she leaned over him. He was stretched out on a narrow camp-bed in a small back room of the Double Five ranch house.

'Feels bad enough as it is — name's Ross, by the way.'

'Yes, I know,' she said, smiling and tightening the bandage around his upper left arm, reaching so she could pass it around his chest a few times before tying it off, restricting movement. She straightened and did that thing he'd noticed before: it was a kind of sweeping motion that pushed rebellious chestnut

177

hair back into place above her eyes. The hair was naturally wavy and likely could have benefited from some kind of pin to hold it. He'd had the thought before, even on their brief first acquaintance, that Dana was an easy-going outdoor girl and, while she wouldn't allow any degree of slovenliness in her appearance, didn't care too much about what folk thought of the way she dressed.

'Like to give Stew and Hank some kind of reward.'

'Feel free to offer it, but you may not get them to take it. I employ decent men and most of my crew have been with me for years. It's the code of the range to help anyone in need, in any case. Comes a day when *you* could be the one needing help, you see . . . '

He nodded curtly, rubbing gently at the bandage she had applied. 'You tend to forget decent urges in a place like Yuma. They can even get you whipped — even killed.'

She sobered as she gathered up the first-aid things. 'Yes, I do tend to forget the hardships you've been through.'

'Past now,' he said, maybe a trifle curtly, but not meaning to be short with her. 'I owe you a lot. The whole Double Five, I guess.'

'Let me put some iodine on that cut above your eye and you have one on the side of your jaw that looks like it really should've been stitched.'

'Doc Sheehan mentioned it. But it'll heal — Ouch! That iodine stings!'

She smiled and it lit up her whole tanned face. 'And here I was thinking how stalwart and brave you are, not complaining about all your injuries, but you yell your head off with a little sting from iodine!'

He smiled stiffly. 'You want to hear me really yell my head off — well, I'd stuff some rag in my ears first if I was you . . . '

'You must get some rest,' she said with a smile. 'But not too much: it's been my experience that men who've had a physical battering, like you, benefit from some sort of mild exercise

179

as soon as they feel fit enough to attempt it — and that will only come after rest. I'm sure Doc Sheehan would agree.'

'You want some wood chopped for the kitchen? A mustang broken in? Part of the house painted? I'm your man.'

'You are not!' she said emphatically and then flushed a little. 'I mean, I wouldn't dream of allowing you to tackle such things so soon — Oh! You're joshing me, of course!' She drew down a deep breath and there was some annoyance in the look she gave him. 'If you rest well tonight and feel like it after breakfast, we'll go riding and you can see just what a wild ride you must've survived coming down the creek to the point where it merges with the river. That's where Stew and Hank found you.'

He nodded and, as she made to leave, reached up and lightly grabbed her left wrist. She looked down at him sharply.

'Thanks, Dana, you'll never know

how much I appreciate this.'

'I thought I explained — '

'You did. But thanks anyway. I have to tell you, someone'll get that posse free pretty soon and I — They may blame me for killing Sheriff Fuller. I didn't do it. It was Lee Connor: I give you my word.'

She squeezed his hand as she gently lifted it from her wrist. 'Then that's good enough for me.'

He frowned as she left and closed the door quietly behind her. He felt kind of . . . queer. It had been so long — *hell, all the time he was in jail!* — since anyone had really listened to him, readily taken his word as he pleaded innocence of incidents a lot less serious than murder.

He was battered and sore and tired, but just thinking about the subject — and Dana — kept him awake half the night.

★   ★   ★

He bathed in a tin hip-bath of hot, sudsy water before breakfast and was surprised at the amount of food he put away at the long table in the bunkhouse afterwards.

The crew numbered eleven as far as he could make out, though the remuda was big enough for twice that many ranch hands. They were boisterous and sullen and yawning, some even half-asleep, as they shovelled flapjacks and cornpone into their stubbled faces. There were lots of stares, the occasional friendly nod, the odd hostile glare.

Seemed about par for the course, he reckoned.

Dana rode a big white mare and had chosen a high-stepping sorrel gelding for McCall.

'If he's too big for a start,' she began to apologize as he made a couple of awkward attempts to reach the high stirrup.

'No! It's me. Stiff 'n' sore, is . . . *all!*' This last was said with gusto as he finally swung up and settled in the saddle. The horse didn't seem to mind.

And, as he set the reins to the length he wanted, he noticed the Winchester in the scabbard on his saddle.

'I thought you might appreciate the company,' she told him.

He patted the rifle butt as they rode slowly across the busy yard with men noisily selecting work-mounts for the day, dust and curses alike coming from the corrals.

'Old friends, Mr Winchester and me. Obliged, Dana, for everything you've done.'

She just gave him a slight nod and he noticed she carried a carbine in her own scabbard and had a small .32-calibre revolver in an embossed holster around her waist.

They rode through some of her herds and, when they reached the south pasture, he glanced up to the bastions of Dark Mesa towering above.

'I think it might be as well if you stayed away from there for a short time,' she suggested.

'I'll give it some thought. Nothing much left up there for anyone to wreck or burn now — thanks to this Moreno. You know him?'

Ranging alongside as they were forced to turn away from the mesa by a patch of heavy brush, she shook her head.

'I've heard of him. Some sort of . . . speculator, in land and construction. One of those extremely rich men who never seem to accumulate enough money. He speculates with other people's cash and somehow manages to grab the biggest percentage for himself, though I have heard he was heading for a financial fall. He's a very powerful man, nevertheless. Some say a *frightening* man.'

Sober now, McCall nodded. 'More or less the picture I've got of him. But damned if I know what he wants of me. Oh, I guess it could be the Wells Fargo hold-up money, but I can't help him there — no idea where it is.'

'You may have a difficult job

convincing him of that,' she said quietly.

'Mebbe, if we ever get to meet.'

A rifle shot whip-cracking through the draws to their left cut him short. And then Dana made a gasping sound and he watched in horror as she jerked violently and toppled from the saddle.

She sprawled in some grass and McCall was off his horse in a flash, slipping the Winchester from the scabbard, searching for the gunman. He glimpsed movement in some brush high up on the lip of a draw, threw the rifle to his shoulder and fired three rapid shots. As the echoes died he froze.

A rough, amused voice called down. 'Save your ammo, McCall! I hear you ain't got many friends, but you're gonna lose 'em all, one by one, you don't come to your senses. You can cross off Fuller, an' that old sawbones won't be no trouble pretty soon, an' — But you know what I mean, huh? Make a friend, he becomes a target!'

'I know, you sonofabitch!' McCall recognized Lee Connor's voice. 'And when I catch up with you, I'm gonna make sure *you* savvy just why I'm gonna kill you! And it won't be quick!'

Connor laughed. 'Nasty old prison habits, huh? Well, we'll see . . . For now, I was you I'd look to the gal! I aimed just to wound, but there's a crosswind and, well, you never know, mighta made a mistake!'

McCall cursed: the bastard was right! He was wasting time that would be better spent helping Dana.

Heart pounding, half-expecting a bullet in the back, he ran to where the girl lay, very still. The big horse was sniffing curiously around a fresh splash of red trickling from under her left side on to a patch of green grass.

13

A Toast in Bourbon

Doc Sheehan wasted no time in examining Dana's wound when McCall brought her in, sweating, dust-covered.

'It's low down, in or under the arch of the left ribs, Doc.'

'Get out of the way, man! Let me see for myself.'

They were in the doctor's surgery and Mrs Sheehan was there in a long white calico coat that had seen the washtub dozens of times, by the looks of it. She was a severe-faced woman with her grey hair piled up in a bun on top of her head. She glared at McCall through *pince-nez*, shifted focus and looked at him over the tops of the lenses.

'You got her shot.' It was a flat accusation — and unforgiving.

'Yes, ma'am. It was because of me. They're trying to make me do what they want by shooting my friends now. It — '

'Will you wait outside!' snapped the medic impatiently. He glared at his wife. 'Get him out of here, then come back and lend a hand.'

She didn't look like the type who would take kindly to that tone, but it was obvious she was a practical woman: she took McCall's uninjured arm in a surprisingly iron grip and marched him out into a dim waiting room.

'We'll call you if we need you.'

'Will you let me know as soon as she's all right? Or . . . if she isn't?'

'Find yourself an old newspaper and be patient.'

She stomped out and he immediately felt lost, but there were some old newspapers from various parts of the country and he tried to settle down and read one.

He'd read three before Sheehan himself opened the door, wiping his hands on a small white towel, clothes covered by a blood-spattered, once-blue linen coat.

'Oh, sit down! She'll be all right after a stay here for a few days. Whoever shot her couldn't have done a better job. The bullet passed between two lower ribs and went on to make only an unusually small exit hole. I would say the bullet itself had been filed to a needle point to do that.'

'He wasn't trying to kill her, Doc; it was a warning — to me. From Connor.'

The doctor glanced at him sharply, frowning, then nodded gently. 'I see. His idea of pressure, I take it.'

'Showing me just what he can do whenever he likes, unless *I* do what he wants.'

'D'you know what that is?'

'No, Doc. I still dunno what Moreno wants of me but I aim to find out.'

'You do have other troubles, you know.' At McCall's puzzled look, he added, 'Town blacksmith, Simm Barcross, managed to get out of that dead-end canyon where you marooned the posse. There are men up there now trying to blast a way out for them and their horses. Simm says Connor claims you shot Rafe Fuller.'

'The hell I did!' McCall told how it had happened, and how he had seen a big man who could have been Barcross when Connor was holding him under his gun. 'Connor forced me to make a run for it with him: Barcross must've seen that. But I ended up in that damn creek.'

'Well, that can be sorted out later. Let me look at that arm. Dana's done a good job of restricting movement and you'd do well to use it as little as possible.'

'It's the other arm I aim to use, Doc.'

'Your gun arm,' Doc said, with a hint of disapproval.

'You haven't got a six-gun I could borrow, have you?'

'As a matter of fact I have several. Relics of some of my patients who never made it through various medical complications . . . and occasionally, by the way of payment. You're welcome to choose one or more.'

* * *

Virgil Caldwell snapped his head up irritably as his office door crashed open again, and felt his bowels quail as Ross McCall entered, kicking the door closed behind him.

He carried a rifle in one hand, the other obviously restricted by bandages, and there was a holstered Colt at his waist.

'M-my — My God! Wha — What are you doing here?'

The rifle jerked and Caldwell cringed a little in his chair.

'Figured it was time you and me had a talk, Caldwell, about this Moreno and his interest in me.' He rapped the rifle barrel hard on the edge of the desk, causing ink to splash out of a stone well.

'I-I'm sorry. My clients have privilege and I'm unable to discuss — *Aaaaah!*'

He sat back violently as the rifle muzzle pressed up under his jaw, digging in deep, the foresight breaking the skin so a thin trickle of blood ran down to his starched collar. McCall towered above the chair where the attorney half-lay now, eyes wide, sweat beading his flushed face.

'Before we start, I want to tell you I have just taken Dana Cooke to Doc Sheehan, shot in the side by Lee Connor, who seems to have some connection to you.'

Caldwell gagged as he tried to speak and the rifle's pressure eased a little. The attorney shook his head quickly, breath hissing through his flaring nostrils.

'I-I know nothing about Dana Cooke's wounding! I swear!'

'You likely suggested it, you lying sonofabitch!'

Caldwell cringed as McCall took a step closer.

'No, no! Connor's a client only inasmuch as Mr Moreno asked him to do a certain . . . chore. I-I was hired in a secondary capacity to, well, smooth the way for Connor, I suppose is the best way to put it.'

'Might be the best for you and your fancy lawyer ways, but for me' — McCall leaned forward, eyes bleak — 'it better be explained in plain words — briefly — *and now!*'

'G-Give me a minute to collect myself, please! I'm not used to having guns waved in my face.'

There was a clock encased in a glass dome on the end of Caldwell's large desk. McCall reached for it with his injured hand and almost dropped it.

'Careful! That's a genuine Marchant-Cussons! Oh, I see by your face you're not familiar with antiques, well — My God! Don't do that!'

McCall let the clock fall but managed to catch it before it hit the corner of the desk — just. 'Your minute's ticking away, mister.'

That was Caldwell's last attempt at delay. Voice trembling, reaching cautiously into a drawer to bring out a bundle of papers tied with pink tape and a wax seal, he began to speak. 'You may find this file I've kept of interest . . .'

* * *

Doc Sheehan came out of the room where Dana had been placed, tugging down his shirtsleeves. He stopped when he saw McCall standing across the hall, rifle pointing to the floor, looking drawn and very tired.

'Here, I think I'd best prescribe some of my special medicine for you. Come into my office.'

'I don't want any medicine, Doc.'

'Not even three-year-old bonded bourbon from Kentucky? Genuine, I assure you.'

McCall shrugged. 'Not much of a drinker, Doc, but mebbe I can do with a belt of some kinda hooch.'

'That's no way to speak about this bourbon! Here, try it and — Good grief, man! You don't toss it down like a ten-cent redeye in the saloon! You appreciate it by — '

'Doc, the whiskey hits the spot. I don't care about its history. Before we get to talkin', how is Dana?'

'Still sleeping, of course. She'll sleep right through the night, I hope.' He took a sip of his own drink, rolling it around his mouth before swallowing, smacking his lips and smiling. 'Fine bourbon! The finest — '

McCall shrugged impatiently. 'Did you know Ace Morgan very well, Doc?'

Sheehan looked suddenly wary. 'Er, perhaps quite a little — quite a *deal*, better than most law-abiding folk.'

McCall smiled slowly. 'Yeah, according to Caldwell, Ace was your half-brother. That true?'

The medic sighed. 'Yes, an indiscretion on the part of someone in the family. We were never close, but he used my expertise with gunshot wounds once or twice, though I have to admit he didn't take undue advantage of me. He still has something to do with your present troubles?'

'According to Caldwell, who appears to be suffering something like a nervous breakdown at the moment. Can't seem to stop talking.'

'I see.'

'No you don't, Doc, but it's not important. He's just had a sort of bad fright, I guess you'd call it. I believe he's leaving town on the next stage.'

Sheehan smiled thinly. 'Perhaps I see more than you think.'

'Doc, I'm tired of all this. That damned Wells Fargo loot has been hanging over my head for too blamed long.'

'You're not thinking of going up against a man like Moreno!'

'He's going up agin me! And I've had a bellyful. Caldwell has been nosing around in Moreno's affairs more than he ought to and now he's scared, on the verge of full-blown panic, but he claims that details of a soil analysis of the mesa cap were in the same satchel as the Wells Fargo payroll, in a smaller and securely locked special delivery leather bag for important letters. Seems it's a common method used by business folk, at extra charge of course, to make sure their confidential papers arrive safely, carried in the famous Wells Fargo strongbox instead of just a regular mailbag.'

Doc arched his bushy eyebrows quizzically. 'I believe I've heard of that service offered by Wells Fargo.'

'It's from Excelsior Mineral Exploration Company.'

He waited. The doctor stared at him levelly. 'I believe Moreno holds shares in that company.'

'He arranged for a mineral survey for silver-lead in that dark soil capping the mesa at its north end.'

'That cap is very large! If it proved to be rich in silver ore, why, you could buy Mexico, or half-a-dozen of those European so-called kingdoms! It would have tremendous value!'

'Even to a greedy sonofabitch like Moreno?'

The sawbones looked thoughtful. 'Ye-es! I think even he would be willing to wait a few years to get his hands on something like that.'

'If it turned out to be as rich as he hoped.'

Sheehan snapped his head up. 'If it proved to be rich in silver? Are you saying — ?'

'It's rich, but mostly in lead. Quite valuable to your regular run-of-the-mill prospector, but to a man who thinks in multi-thousands like Moreno . . . ' He shrugged, spreading his hands. 'Peanuts. Lead wouldn't be worth his time, but silver would be another matter.'

'Let me get this clear: are you saying the cap contains more lead than silver?'

'Appears so. I learned some of this stuff by reading about it in Noah Webster's *Dictionary*. The two minerals are often found together and lead often dominates. Caldwell had an analysis done for himself, afraid Moreno wouldn't cut him in on the deal, I guess.'

'Sounds very much like Virgil.'

'Well, it turns out there is a much bigger percentage of lead than silver, enough to make any grubline prospector drool, mebbe, but not someone like Moreno.'

'Nor a prospective backer?'

'Right, Doc. That's his problem. He speculated with other people's money and it seems a lot of his speculations crashed in the last couple of years, and particularly in the last six months, not just here, but overseas. He's managed to cover up by borrowing new money, stalling everyone off, but now he needs hard cash before those big city boys start banging on his door and demanding their money back. He's already received several threats.'

'And they'd be interested in a mesaful of silver?'

'Something like that would pull him out of the hole he's in, and it's a deep one, according to Caldwell. Those big city financiers live and breathe dollars and cents. And Moreno's way behind with his repayments. The lenders seem to have decided it's gone far enough, so he has to come up with the money — and fast.'

'Caldwell found all this out? I mean, I'm not surprised he could do it, only that he *would* do it. Doesn't seem the type to tangle with someone like Moreno.'

'You'd be surprised at how the good ol' dollar can put backbone into a greedy weakling, Doc. Yuma's full of such fools.'

'Yes, I can imagine, but Moreno?'

'He had some forger make up a fake report, telling how the mesa cap was *mighty* rich in *silver*. You can't tell the report from the genuine article, and with that and Moreno's past reputation, they took a chance, loaned him hundreds of thousands. A stopgap only, for him, but that's how his type work: they keep bluffing, hoping to pull off another big coup. Like a gambler in debt over cards. The new loan was sent out by a special delivery letter of credit, carried in that satchel with the Wells Fargo payroll, very secure. *Delivery guaranteed*, unless someone like

Ace Morgan grabs it halfway.'

'So Moreno had backing he needed because of his past performances for a silver mine that could never exist, and he can't get his hands on it!' Doc pursed his lips. 'By now, some of those financiers must be getting edgy waiting for a return on their investment.'

'Well, he must've stalled them somehow, because he's still in business and, for now anyway, they're going along with his excuses for delays in getting started on mining the silver.'

'So-called speculators are noted for their expertise at stalling impatient creditors, I've heard.'

'Then Ace Morgan shows up, wounded and on the run, with the satchel carrying the Wells Fargo payroll and the special delivery letter, hides it somewhere on the mesa, and nobody can find it. Those hard boys from back East must be ready to teach Moreno a mighty hard lesson — even look at putting him out of business permanently. No money, but a warning for anyone else they might deal with.'

'And Moreno's convinced you know where the satchel is hidden, with all that cash just waiting for him to use, and save his neck!'

McCall held up a hand quickly. 'Everyone *figures* I know where Ace hid the satchel, but fact is he never had a chance to tell me before the posse got him. Only a general area he'd been in.'

Sheehan nodded soberly. 'And . . . ?'

McCall gave him a crooked smile in reply. 'Naturally, I poked around, took me a long time, hunting through Arrowhead Draw, but I covered every damn foot of it. I think maybe I found where Ace stashed it, but someone had been there before me.' He paused. 'And got richer by a hundred thousand dollars.'

The medic spluttered his top-level whiskey around half the office, coughed and wiped his wet chin and tears from his eyes as he stared at McCall. 'Only if they didn't mind risking using stolen money!'

McCall held his gaze steadily. 'Moreno

thinks I'm holding out on him, that I have the money; that's why he keeps pushing at me.'

'I don't envy your position!'

'Why did you tell me about Moreno's name, Doc? You know, meaning 'dark', as if the mesa was named after Moreno and not the big fire during the Indian Wars?'

Sheehan cleared his throat, busying himself at pouring himself another whiskey. McCall covered his glass with his hand. 'The Morenos can trace their family back to the *Conquistadors*. In those days, they saw a piece of land they liked, they took it, settled it, built it up. The Spanish are very strong on family as you probably know. Having land was and is very important to them.'

He sipped his whiskey, stood and walked around the room to a window, spoke again while looking out.

'The Morenos became quite powerful, acquired huge tracts of land, including the mesa — even called it Moreno Mesa, but the *Americanos* were moving in by that time, taking over their own country, so to speak, and they didn't care for a Spanish name on a landmark like the mesa, so they took the English meaning of *Moreno* — *dark* — and renamed it.'

'Did Moreno try to reclaim it for his family?'

'Oh, yes, but at that time, he had more failures than successes with his speculations and eventually had to turn over the mesa to the US authorities, even though he'd been living there for some years.'

'So he'd know the mesa pretty well, maybe even the best hiding places for a satchel full of stolen money?'

'Yup. And, knowing Moreno, I'm sure he searched thoroughly. It'd be hard to decide whether he wants the money to pay off his backers who are stirring rather dangerously, or he wants to use it to buy back the mesa on behalf of the Moreno family.' He frowned suddenly. 'But he is apparently very short of cash and keeps harassing you, so he may well believe you *haven't* yet found the satchel.'

'Well, Doc, he's like most folk around here: he believes I know where the satchel's hidden and by rousting me, he's showing what he's capable of and it could get a whole lot worse if I don't hand it over.'

'But then again, with someone like Willard Moreno, you can't be sure of anything.'

Doc Sheehan suddenly raised his glass.

'To good ol' *greed*! May it choke the life out of its disciples!' He drank deeply again, saw that McCall hadn't touched his glass. 'Don't you feel like celebrating?'

'What I feel like doing, Doc, is going after Lee Connor, and when I finish with him, square up to Señor Moreno.'

Sheehan looked sober now. 'Oh, that's a very foolish move, Ross! Very foolish — and very, very dangerous!'

'Mebbe, but it has to be done, Doc.'

The sawbones frowned and then nodded slowly.

'Ye-es, I see that; to a man like you, it *will* have to be done no matter what the risk.' He lifted the bottle more sedately towards his mouth now. 'To your success.'

McCall smiled briefly, reached for his glass.

'I'll drink to that.'

14

Meet the Enemy

McCall was determined now to get this deal over and done with. He busied himself readying his mount for a long trail, cleaned and oiled his guns carefully, testing them several times before he was satisfied.

Around mid-morning he went to see Dana Cooke.

She was conscious and looked pale, but gave him a hesitant smile when Mrs Sheehan, scowling, reluctantly showed him into her room.

'You have ten minutes, young man,' the doctor's wife told McCall and he nodded, held the door until she realized he was waiting for her to leave. She made a small *Humpff* and left. He closed the door, turned and found Dana's smile had widened some.

'She means well.' Her voice was husky but strong enough.

'Never mind her. I'll be going away for a while and just wanted to check on you before I left.'

Alarm showed on her pale face as she struggled to sit up a little more. He hurried and arranged the pillows to suit. Her hand fumbled at his forearm, her grip quite weak.

'You're not going after Moreno?'

'Have to, Dana, he's forcing my hand. I've had enough, especially when my friends start getting shot because of me.'

'Oh, Ross! Don't be silly! You're one man and Moreno can call on — well, I don't know how many men, but I'm sure you'll be outnumbered.'

'Expect to be. But I know a few tricks and I'll track him down and force a showdown.'

'I-I wish you wouldn't, Ross!'

'The only way I know.'

Her hazel eyes roamed his face and she managed to tighten her grip on his forearm a little as she nodded slowly. 'Yes, I believe that. I know I can't stop you, but do your best to come back to me — safely — please?'

When he left shortly afterward he was ready to take on the world. *More than ready!*

Dana wanted him to come back to her!

It would take more than someone like Moreno and Connor to stop him doing just that.

★ ★ ★

The Lambert Ridge stage made an ungainly swing around the hairpin bend and the driver, half-standing, whip flicking at the sweat-gleaming rumps of the team so as to straighten up the vehicle quickly, suddenly swore, sat down with a thump, hauling on the reins. There were startled cries from inside, the tumble of hand luggage — *and* passengers — as well as the shriek of the brakes clasping and smoking on the iron-tyred wheels as the stage shuddered to a halt.

With thudding heart, the driver stared at the horseman sitting squarely across the narrow trail, rifle butt on his thigh, finger on the trigger, the hammer at full cock.

'Howdy, Batwing, won't delay you long, just want a word or two with one of your passengers.'

'By God! *I'll* give *you* a word or two, McCall!'

'Likely heard 'em all.' McCall touched his heels to his horse's flanks and walked it up alongside the dusty stage where passengers were arguing and cussing. He fired a shot into the air, quickly jacked another shell into the breech.

'Counsellor Caldwell, step down, please.'

'McCall, you are makin' one helluva lot of trouble for yourself! Disruptin' the stageline schedule, kidnappin' one of my passengers — '

Batwing closed his mouth with a snap as the rifle swung towards him. 'Drive on, Batwing, you've only lost a couple of minutes.'

'I can't leave one of my passengers with you!'

'Not gonna keep him. Just have a short talk. You stop at that bluff yonder — not quite a mile — and when I finish my talk with the counsellor he can walk out to you.'

'In this heat!' croaked the white-faced Caldwell.

'You could do with losing a little weight.'

There was no levity in McCall now and Batwing figured he better get going. As he lifted the reins he said, 'Still gonna report this!'

'*Adios*, Batwing.' The rifle cracked again, echoes slapping flatly, as the stage rolled on and Caldwell started to yell and wave his arms.

'Shut up, Counsellor. You talk again, you better be ready to tell me where I'll find Connor and this damn Moreno! How about it?'

Caldwell swung his gaze after the dwindling stage and its plume of dust, then licked his lips and spoke in a croaking voice. 'Moreno has a *hacienda* outside of Zapata Springs. Colorado.'

'Sticking to the old *Conquistador* country, huh? And Lee Connor?'

Although he was trembling and kept watching the stagecoach, Caldwell suddenly tried to grin, but it looked kind of sickly. 'Well, well, I wouldn't be surprised if you met *him* somewhere along the trail. Though you mightn't hear the shot he'll fire at you!' He cringed, sick at his own temerity. 'He saw you leaving my office and I had to tell him why you were there. I thought it inadvisable for me to stay.'

'For once I think you're telling the truth, Counsellor.' McCall manoeuvred his horse closer and Caldwell got ready to run. 'Climb up behind and I'll save you a hot walk.'

Caldwell's shaky legs almost gave way as he reached up, sucking in great breaths at his sudden salvation.

* * *

Connor was likely smart enough to know that McCall would not allow Caldwell to clear town without getting more information from the man, and would have to stop the stage to do this.

McCall didn't really expect Connor to be watching at this point, but was unwilling to take the chance.

Caldwell himself hadn't quite recovered from his shock at being able to clamber aboard the coach to Lambert Ridge again, unharmed. As McCall turned his mount to ride away when the impatient Batwing whipped up the team, Caldwell leaned out of the window and called in a shaky voice, 'He told me he prefers a dry wash where he can shoot down on his target.'

Ross McCall waved, surprised, but willing to take Caldwell's word now: he had already figured that Connor was a man experienced in ambush.

If he was watching the stage, Connor would know Caldwell would tell everything, including the kind of ambush site he favoured.

* * *

Even so, McCall missed the first suitable ambush draw, and later reckoned he was mighty lucky Connor *hadn't* been there or he could be dead by now.

When he saw the second dry wash coming up — mighty hard to discern with the dust pall kicked up by the stagecoach — McCall decided he could use that dust as cover.

He spurred his mount and ran it into a thick part of the swirling cloud, tugging up his neckerchief over mouth and nose.

If Connor was waiting, he would be high up on the rim and, as the rim of the wash dipped downward, too, it gave any bushwhacker a good advantage, shooting from above. *Just the way Connor liked it,* according to Caldwell.

And now was the time he would find out for sure whether the attorney had been telling the truth, or had outsmarted him and sent him to his death.

He squinted in the clouds of dust and grit that whipped back from the narrow walls due to the passage of the stage and took some comfort in the knowledge that if he couldn't get a clear look at the rim above him, Connor probably wouldn't have a good view of him down in amongst all this fog and scud.

Then a bullet smacked through the brim of his hat, knocking it sideways on his head. He didn't hesitate: he yanked hard on the reins, twisting the startled mount's head around as he threw his weight into the move. The horse whinnied and snorted and plunged, eventually reared, and he felt himself going backwards out of the saddle.

He let himself fall, kicking boots out of the stirrups, using the brief support of the irons to drive his body over the frightened animal's rump. He landed hard, covering his head instinctively, and felt a hoof graze his flesh as it ripped through his shirtsleeve.

He rolled in close to the wall, heard

the rifle above him hammering shot after shot down into the dust cloud. Choking and spitting mud, he worked knees, boots and shoulders, squirming under the slight overhang. The horse ran on, no doubt terrified by now.

He hit his head on a rock and blinked away the whirling stars, squinting. Up there, against the hot blue of the sky, the rim was little more than a smudge seen through the murk but he spotted Connor.

The man was standing amongst some rocks, leaning out, straining to see if McCall was still in the saddle or maybe being dragged with a boot caught in the stirrup. McCall threw his rifle to his shoulder and worked lever and trigger in a roaring three-shot volley.

A thick pall of dust rolled in and he swore as it prevented him from even making out the hazy outline of Connor above. Then the bushwhacker's rifle answered him and bullets kicked dust and grit over his shoulders. He twisted violently, dropped to one knee, and triggered two more shots: there was so much gun-smoke and dust now he couldn't even see the edge of the rim let alone his target. He ran left a couple of yards, stopped abruptly as Connor's rifle cracked, spun, the Winchester whipping up to his shoulder, and fired.

Rim dirt erupted and, moments later, something dropped from above and he threw himself back even as a flailing arm caught him across the head. Staggering upright and coughing, he made out the dusty, blood-smeared and broken body of Lee Connor, pinning one of his legs.

McCall eased his legs from under the weight and sat back against the wall of the dry wash, his heart thundering.

One down, how many to go?

There was only one way to find out.

* * *

It took him four days to reach Zapata Springs.

The town was larger than he expected,

had a definite Spanish influence, with lots of white adobe buildings, a church with a tall bell tower. Many of the citizens wore Spanish-style clothing. There were plenty of *Americanos*, too, so he was able to ride in quietly and mingle with some of the population. Later, he haunted American-style saloons rather than cantinas, though he might well need to visit the latter to get information about Señor Felipe Bernalillio Moreno, as he was known here. *The Don*. 'Willard' was a name he used when he was playing stock markets and land deals.

McCall needn't have worried about locating him: for the price of a few beers and a bottle of mescal he learnt that Don Felipe Moreno had his *hacienda* three miles north of town, on a huge area of nigh on a thousand acres, patrolled by armed men night and day.

He got directions and with dire warnings ringing in his ears rode out to find this small kingdom that seemed impregnable. He camped high in the sierras and scanned the place inch by inch with a pair of good-quality army field-glasses. He made notes of times when obvious guards appeared and where, although there were nowhere near as many as he might have expected after what he had heard in town.

But they were all heavily armed and looked very businesslike.

The easiest thing to do would have been for McCall to set himself up on some ridge with his rifle and a telescopic sight, then pick Moreno off at his leisure.

But that wasn't his way.

He wanted to come face to face with this sonofabitch who believed the entire world revolved about him and his desires. Put *honestly*, he wanted to kill this man who had callously ordered Dana Cooke to be shot so as to put pressure on *him*, and also burned down his almost completed cabin just to make him tell the location of the satchel with the Wells Fargo money.

But in his cautious queries in town he had several hints that Señor Moreno was a mighty worried man. Following through, he learned that he was in very deep financial trouble, his funds fast dwindling, his backers demanding he pay what he owed them: his deadline was fast approaching.

The money-lenders were men who would not stand for anyone failing to meet their obligations. The way they operated, it just wasn't possible to allow anyone to get away with such a thing. Rather than compromise and perhaps make arrangements for the debt to be repaid a little at a time, they chose — always — to make an example of the debtor. *Kill him and bear the loss!* A brutal lesson for others which seemed to work surprisingly well.

To such men, this was far more acceptable than showing any leniency, which they regarded as 'softness' and a threat to future operations.

McCall pieced together his snippets of information and reached the conclusion that Don Felipe Moreno was living on borrowed time.

Briefly, there was the thought that all he had to do was sit back and allow the hardcases from back East to do the job for him. *Easy! And safe.*

But this was personal and *had to be settled his way!*

So, where did that leave him: money fast running out, constantly aware that he might draw attention to himself and be killed out of hand simply to protect Moreno from any possible threat? And he was alone.

But he was damned if he would resort to ambush, sneaking away afterwards like some animal. Whatever he did might be hard to live with, but *he had to tell Moreno to his face that he was not God. Had to!*

Then, on his way back to his room one night, perhaps with one too many tequilas under his belt, he heard a sound behind him, stopped and turned, stumbling slightly as he felt for his Colt.

Moving shadows rushing towards him!

The first man was almost upon him

but he brought up his Colt and smashed it into the dark face. There was a choking cry and the man dropped out of sight. A gun blasted close by and the impact of the sound set his head buzzing, throwing his balance, which likely saved him from another bullet as a second gun roared.

He was down on his knees now, brought his Colt across in front of his body and used the edge of his left hand to fan the hammer, shooting into the tight-packed group.

He emptied his gun — three or four shots — and heard screams. A man yelled something unintelligible in a high-pitched voice and there were sudden sounds of men skidding as they turned about, desperate to get away now.

As he fumbled fresh cartridges out of his belt loops, something slammed across his skull, knocking off his battered hat. Fireworks exploded briefly in his head before they were abruptly extinguished as there was another jarring blow before he plunged into blackness.

★ ★ ★

He thought it was still night when he started to come round, but if he turned his head at a certain angle, there was a sliver of what could only be sunlight at the edge of the blindfold he wore.

Blindfold! Seconds later he realized his wrists were bound in his lap, and his ankles held firmly against the rough legs of a wooden chair. He was surprised to find that the groaning sounds came from his own lips.

'Bring the *don*,' a voice said in Spanish. 'This *perro* joins us again.'

There were sounds of someone leaving in a hurry and then his throbbing head was wrenched back hard enough to make him grunt as a bottle neck crushed his lips against his teeth. He gagged as he was forced to swallow the fiery liquid that filled his mouth. The bottle was removed and he coughed and gagged. A hard hand cuffed him across the head.

'*Silencio!*' the voice barked.

He could hear people moving about, a door opening and closing, voices speaking in Spanish too rapid for him to savvy. Then he felt the presence of someone standing very close before him and suddenly the blindfold was ripped off, making him wince as tears flowed. He blinked, had the impression of four or five men in a mostly bare, lantern-lit room with stone walls. They stepped aside quickly, allowing a short man in rich-looking clothes embroidered in the Spanish way, and with a sabre at his waist in a gold-filigreed sheath, to reach out and twist his fingers in McCall's hair. His head was yanked back painfully, and a swarthy face with a dark, goatee beard, and winey breath, growled, 'So this is the one! McCall!' The short man spat on him and leaned down, his face only inches from the prisoner's. 'You have caused me a great deal of trouble, Señor McCall. I realize now I have wasted my time. I should have had you brought here in the first place where we could work on you at our leisure — and where your screams would not be heard outside these walls.'

'If you're hoping I can tell you where to find that Wells Fargo satchel, you're outa luck. Don — you *puerco!*'

Hard knuckles cracked against his face, filling his mouth with blood and almost overturning the chair.

'There is no longer time to negotiate!' Moreno snapped in his heavily accented English. 'I need that money! *I must have it and quickly!*'

'Comin' after you, are they, *amigo?*' McCall managed to slur, tasting his own blood in his swollen mouth. 'Pay up or die? Hell, I thought you were s'posed to be such a hard *hombre* that no one could get to you — '

He gasped the last two words as a big Mexican with a stubbled face slapped him silly with a rapid barrage of blows to his body and head. Blood dripped on to his bound hands as he lifted his battered face.

'Can't you get it through your *thick* head that *I dunno where the goddamn*

225

satchel is? My mesa's been dug up to hell and gone in places; looks like someone's ready to plant a couple thousand flowers in it! *Someone* must've found it while I was still in Yuma — and that's gospel. Do whatever you like to me, b-but that's all I can tell you!'

The big Mexican started to hit him again. Moreno lifted a hand quickly. The *don* looked pale, wary, but with a strange concentration that told McCall, even in his semi-conscious state, that the Spaniard was — reluctantly! — almost ready to believe him.

'You think I wouldn't've had my ranch built by now if I'd found that loot?' he mumbled.

Then a slow smile crossed Moreno's face. 'No, I do not think so, McCall. Why? Because you are one of those stupid *Americanos* who, because the money was stolen, would declare it to your authorities and end up with *nothing!* Or, at most, a pittance by way of a reward.'

He threw up his hands and let go a

string of Spanish oaths, then, breathless, he rounded on McCall.

'I may actually believe you, McCall, but you must see I cannot take the chance you are speaking the truth. *I have to know*, so I must torture you until I am certain.'

'I'm not stupid, Moreno. I don't look forward to your damn torture, but *I don't know where that money is!* Half of Keystone dug up my mesa looking for it. Someone must've found it! And kept quiet . . . likely moved away.'

Moreno stopped the big Mexican once more from beating McCall. 'Carlos, it is possible he might be telling the truth, but go set up your pincers and hot needles and knives. We will get this over with quickly.' He gestured to one of the men to cut McCall's legs free but to leave his hands tied in front of him.

Roughly hauled to his feet, he swayed drunkenly, afraid his legs were going to collapse under him. The guards grinned and poked and pushed him from one to the other, laughing as they staggered him, making him even more dizzy.

Looking annoyed, Don Felipe snapped to the big Carlos, 'When will my coach arrive?'

'Any time now, Don Felipe. They are just provisioning it for your journey back to Mexico.'

Moreno sighed, glanced around the room. 'Such a pity! To leave all I have built up over the years. I will miss the *emoción*, the excitement, but — Aah! Is that the coach arriving now?' McCall dimly heard the clatter of a vehicle somewhere outside.

Carlos frowned and said slowly, 'I believe so, Don Felipe, but . . . it is early. I ordered it not to come here until I sent word. I thought you would like to watch at least some of the *tormentos* we have prepared for this pig.'

He prodded McCall hard in the ribs and Ross gagged, doubled over. Then there was sudden shouting and a volley of gunshots. Carlos drew a big pistol and stepped in front of Moreno, protecting him with his large body. The Spaniard clapped a hand to the hilt of his sabre, half-drew it from the scabbard, then swung a baleful look at the still grimacing McCall.

There was a ragged volley of gun-shots which brought guards and all to their toes, most glancing in the direction of the *don*, who looked suddenly pale beneath his swarthiness.

Shouting, he ordered the other men in the room to get guns as the door crashed open and four *gringos* charged in. The leader was a medium-tall man with a smoking pistol in each hand. He ignored the other Mexicans and stepped right up to Carlos, rammed a gun barrel up under his jaw and pulled the trigger before the big Mexican could bring up his own weapon.

Then he lifted the pistol in his other hand and swung towards Moreno. The Spaniard stepped behind McCall, who was straightening now, swung his sabre up towards his throat.

'Stop! Or he loses his head!'

'You'll die before it happens, you scum!'

The *gringo*, a middle-aged man, had Moreno's full attention now. McCall held his breath, hands still bound but in front of his body, tingling with returning feeling. Half-closing his eyes, he cut loose with a wild rebel yell close to Moreno's ear. The Spaniard floundered, regained balance and swung with the sabre as McCall rammed his shoulder against him. He felt the sear of the sword's razor edge and prepared to die, but there were three rapid shots from the *gringo*'s gun and Moreno staggered back, dropped to his knees, then fell on his face. The poker-faced *gringo* leaned down casually and put another bullet through his head. Straightening, he looked blandly at McCall. 'Now I know the bastard's dead . . . Here, Ed, cut him loose, get him a decent chair.'

There were still men running across the room, guns hammering, bullets ricocheting dangerously. But then it ended abruptly and there were two *gringos* wounded, three dead Spaniards and two more standing with hands raised.

Hands free now, McCall dabbed at the short cut on his neck, somewhat disconcerted by the way the leader was staring at him.

'You look a mite battered, son, but it's Ross McCall, right?'

'Ye-ah — Aw, hell! Mr Dennison! How the — ?'

'Never did meet officially, did we? Just a nod when I came to pick up Jay.' He paused, cleared his throat. 'I wanted to give you some sort of reward for caring for him in that damn hell-hole in the first stages of the lung fever.'

'Thought it was the usual jail fever, but . . . ' McCall coudn't help but sound apologetic. 'Sorry I couldn't do more.'

'More! Man, you got yourself twenty lashes for stealing some medicine that might've helped Jay! You were only his cellmate, after all, and you risked your neck for him. I tried to get you released after Jay died but someone wanted you kept locked up.'

'So they could search my mesa.'

Dennison nodded, half-smiling. 'Heard about that. But the last few days we heard of a *gringo* named McCall asking questions about Moreno — a man I happened to be interested in. Well, the repayment for helping Jay is somewhat belated but — here we are.'

McCall smiled despite his battered face. 'Welcome!' was all he said.

★ ★ ★

They burned the *hacienda*. The rest of Moreno's men were allowed to scatter to wherever they wished. Without the *don* to back them, they had little or no future in the *Estados Unidos*.

Dennison took McCall to his own *rancho* down in New Mexico, and did a little explaining.

'When Jay died, I was alone. Wife'd died giving birth to Jay, which made him all the more special. He was in jail for some piddling theft he did when he got in with the wrong group. He tell you about it?'

McCall nodded. 'Yes. His mistake was stealing those few bucks from one of Moreno's interests — a whore-house, he told me. Did it on a dare.'

'In the eyes of the law it was theft — full stop.' Dennison sighed. 'Rightly so, I suppose, but, well, it was hard. I thought if I squared the debt, they'd let him go — as you said, it was only a few dollars, but no! That scum, Moreno, wanted to put the screws to me because we'd crossed swords once before. He did me out of money he owed me from one of his speculations. Anyway, we became enemies and when I heard someone named McCall was stirring things up in Moreno's back yard, well, I couldn't ignore that, could I?'

McCall smiled crookedly. 'Glad you didn't. You're a collector? Work for the money men back East, pick up bad debts and so on? I think that's what you told me before, but I was still a mite groggy at the time.'

'That's it, son. Hard work but pays well. Conscience never bothers me. Dirty job, mebbe, but I can live with it. We've been after Moreno for a long time.' Dennison looked levelly at McCall. 'I'd've gladly rescued you for nothing.'

McCall smiled embarrassedly.

'What're you going to do now? There's room for you on my team: lot of travel, fair bit of action if that's your pleasure, or . . . no?'

'Thanks, but no. I'd rather get back to my mesa. There's still a helluva lot to be done there: house to finish, more mavericks for my herds. I'll manage OK now Moreno's no longer in the picture. You don't owe me anything, Mr Dennison.'

'We could differ there but . . . ' He shrugged and looked at him sharply, suddenly snapped his fingers. 'Of course! You've got someone waiting for you! Right?'

McCall nodded. And as he thought of Dana he couldn't help but smile even though his split lips caused him pain.

'Yessir, someone special . . . *very* special.'

Dennison sighed, then held out his hand.

'Best of luck.'

We do hope that you have enjoyed reading this large print book.

Did you know that all of our titles are available for purchase?

We publish a wide range of high quality large print books including:
Romances, Mysteries, Classics
General Fiction
Non Fiction and Westerns

Special interest titles available in large print are:
The Little Oxford Dictionary
Music Book, Song Book
Hymn Book, Service Book

Also available from us courtesy of Oxford University Press:
Young Readers' Dictionary
(large print edition)
Young Readers' Thesaurus
(large print edition)

For further information or a free brochure, please contact us at:
Ulverscroft Large Print Books Ltd.,
The Green, Bradgate Road, Anstey,
Leicester, LE7 7FU, England.
Tel: (00 44) **0116 236 4325**
Fax: (00 44) **0116 234 0205**

Other titles in the
Linford Western Library:

THE HUNT FOR IRON EYES

Rory Black

Iron Eyes is pursuing ruthless outlaws Joe Hyams and Buster Jones. But the pair get the drop on him, and leave him for dead in the dust . . . Meanwhile, another man is on the bounty hunter's trail — gunfighter Wolfe, sworn to take his revenge on the man who left him missing one arm. Kidnapping Squirrel Sally, the woman besotted with Iron Eyes, Wolfe sets off across the prairie — intending to use her as bait to draw out his enemy . . .

THE DEVIL'S ANVIL

Steve Hayes

Two kill-crazy McClory cousins have busted out of Yuma Pen, heading for Indian Territory. Somebody has to bring them in — and the job falls to Deputy US Marshal Liberty Mercer, who sets off to run the outlaws to ground. But to reach the McCrory stronghold in Silver Rock Canyon, Mercer and her makeshift posse — Raven Bjorkman, her old friend; Latham Rawlins, brother of Liberty's one-time love Latigo; and the crooked Dunn brothers — must cross the deadly, searing desert known as the Devil's Anvil . . .

COUGAR TRACKS

Owen G. Irons

Former US Army scout Carroll Cougar desires only to live peacefully on his Twin Creek ranch. Then a letter from the President arrives. Enemy forces plan to assassinate General Crook, and the Army wants Cougar back to take out the threat . . . The old scout has no desire to return to military life. But when he learns that Crook's would-be killer is none other than Solon Reineke, he swiftly saddles up to answer the call of duty. For Reineke is the man who murdered Carlina Polk, a woman Cougar loved . . .

THE TRAIL BREAKERS

Logan Winters

The Broken W ranch has used the same drive route for years: consequentially, every local rustler knows where the herd will pass, making it easy pickings. Ranch owner Glen Wycherly has an old map showing a potential alternative course through the Poconos — however, the map is incomplete. With a contract to deliver five hundred steers to Fort Davis, Wycherly dispatches former railroad man Ray Hardin to survey the new terrain and report back on its suitability. But Hardin and his companion Wally Chambers will find they are riding along a trail of danger . . .

UNION SOLDIER

Gordon Landsborough

In Gin Point, Iowa, the Union Army Enrolment Office is sifting through the locals for recruits. Jim McGaughey, a Harvard-educated doctor far from home, is determined to enlist, despite being exempt from the draft. When one young would-be soldier, roughed up by troopers, goes missing in suspicious circumstances, Jim — now a cavalry trooper — forms an alliance with the youth's sister, who is desperate to discover the truth. But enemies are lurking not only among the Confederates and Sioux, but within the ranks of Jim's blue-coated comrades themselves . . .

STONE OF COURAGE

John Russell Fearn

Abe Jones, nicknamed 'Feather-Fist' for his reluctance to fight, hits the jackpot when panning for gold in a secluded creek. But he is immediately swooped upon by Lynch Corbett and Len Dyson, two of the toughest outlaws in the territory, who drive him off his patch at gunpoint. Sylvia Drew, witness to the event, urges Abe to reclaim what is rightfully his. She reveals to him an ancient Navajo relic known as the Courage Stone — one fragment of which will banish fear and protect the bearer from danger . . .